J.R.R Tolkien.

J.R.R. TOLKIEN

THE LORD OF THE RINGS
comprising:

BOOK ONE
THE RING SETS OUT

BOOK TWO
THE RING GOES SOUTH

BOOK THREE
THE TREASON OF ISENGARD

BOOK FOUR
THE RING GOES EAST

BOOK FIVE
THE WAR OF THE RING

BOOK SIX
THE END OF THE THIRD AGE

and

APPENDICES

APPENDICES

BEING THE FINAL BOOK OF
THE LORD OF THE RINGS

BY

J.R.R. TOLKIEN

An imprint of HarperCollinsPublishers

First published in Great Britain by
George Allen & Unwin 1955
Second edition 1966
This new reset edition published by
HarperCollins*Publishers* 1994
First published in seven volumes 1999
This seven-volume edition 2001

1 3 5 7 9 10 8 6 4 2

Collins is an imprint of HarperCollins*Publishers* Ltd,
77–85 Fulham Palace Road, Hammersmith, London W6 8JB

The HarperCollins website address is
www.**fireandwater**.com

® is a registered trademark of
The J.R.R. Tolkien Estate Limited

www.tolkien.co.uk

ISBN 0 00 763556 7

Printed and bound in Great Britain by
Omnia Books Limited, Glasgow

CONTENTS

Three Rings for the Elven-kings under the sky,
*   Seven for the Dwarf-lords in their halls of stone,*
Nine for Mortal Men doomed to die,
*   One for the Dark Lord on his dark throne*
In the Land of Mordor where the Shadows lie.
*   One Ring to rule them all, One Ring to find them,*
*   One Ring to bring them all and in the darkness bind them*
In the Land of Mordor where the Shadows lie.

APPENDIX A

ANNALS OF THE KINGS AND RULERS

Concerning the sources for most of the matter contained in the following Appendices, especially A to D, see the note at the end of the Prologue. The section A III, *Durin's Folk*, was probably derived from Gimli the Dwarf, who maintained his friendship with Peregrin and Meriadoc and met them again many times in Gondor and Rohan.

The legends, histories, and lore to be found in the sources are very extensive. Only selections from them, in most places much abridged, are here presented. Their principal purpose is to illustrate the War of the Ring and its origins, and to fill up some of the gaps in the main story. The ancient legends of the First Age, in which Bilbo's chief interest lay, are very briefly referred to, since they concern the ancestry of Elrond and the Númenorean kings and chieftains. Actual extracts from longer annals and tales are placed within quotation marks. Insertions of later date are enclosed in brackets. Notes within quotation marks are found in the sources. Others are editorial.[1]

The dates given are those of the Third Age, unless they are marked S.A. (Second Age) or F.A. (Fourth Age). The Third Age was held to have ended when the Three Rings passed away in September 3021, but for the purposes of records in Gondor F.A.I began on March 25, 3021. On the equation of the dating of Gondor and Shire Reckoning see Book I p. 6 and VII p. 113. In lists the dates following the names of kings and rulers are the dates of their deaths, if only one date is given. The sign † indicates a premature death, in battle or otherwise, though an annal of the event is not always included.

---

[1] A few references are given by page to this edition of *The Lord of the Rings*, and to the hardback 4th (reset 4th edition (1995)) edition of *The Hobbit*.

I
THE NÚMENOREAN KINGS

(i)
NÚMENOR

Fëanor was the greatest of the Eldar in arts and lore, but also the proudest and most selfwilled. He wrought the Three Jewels, the *Silmarilli*, and filled them with the radiance of the Two Trees, Telperion and Laurelin,[1] that gave light to the land of the Valar. The Jewels were coveted by Morgoth the Enemy, who stole them and, after destroying the Trees, took them to Middle-earth, and guarded them in his great fortress of Thangorodrim.[2] Against the will of the Valar Fëanor forsook the Blessed Realm and went in exile to Middle-earth, leading with him a great part of his people; for in his pride he purposed to recover the Jewels from Morgoth by force. Thereafter followed the hopeless war of the Eldar and the Edain against Thangorodrim, in which they were at last utterly defeated. The Edain (*Atani*) were three peoples of Men who, coming first to the West of Middle-earth and the shores of the Great Sea, became allies of the Eldar against the Enemy.

There were three unions of the Eldar and the Edain: Lúthien and Beren; Idril and Tuor; Arwen and Aragorn. By the last the long-sundered branches of the Half-elven were reunited and their line was restored.

Lúthien Tinúviel was the daughter of King Thingol Greycloak of Doriath in the First Age, but her mother was Melian of the people of the Valar. Beren was the son of Barahir of the First House of the Edain. Together they wrested a *silmaril* from the Iron Crown of Morgoth.[3] Lúthien became mortal and was lost to Elven-kind. Dior was her son. Elwing was his daughter and had in her keeping the *silmaril*.

Idril Celebrindal was the daughter of Turgon, king of the

---

[1] Cf. II, p. 38; III, p. 249; VI, p. 105: no likeness remained in Middle-earth of Laurelin the Golden.

[2] II. p. 36; IV. p. 150.

[3] I. p. 255; IV, p. 150.

hidden city of Gondolin.[1] Tuor was the son of Huor of the House of Hador, the Third House of the Edain and the most renowned in the wars with Morgoth. Eärendil the Mariner was their son.

Eärendil wedded Elwing, and with the power of the *silmaril* passed the Shadows[2] and came to the Uttermost West, and speaking as ambassador of both Elves and Men obtained the help by which Morgoth was overthrown. Eärendil was not permitted to return to mortal lands, and his ship bearing the *silmaril* was set to sail in the heavens as a star, and a sign of hope to the dwellers in Middle-earth oppressed by the Great Enemy or his servants.[3] The *silmarilli* alone preserved the ancient light of the Two Trees of Valinor before Morgoth poisoned them; but the other two were lost at the end of the First Age. Of these things the full tale, and much else concerning Elves and Men, is told in *The Silmarillion*.

The sons of Eärendil were Elros and Elrond, the *Peredhil* or Half-elven. In them alone the line of the heroic chieftains of the Edain in the First Age was preserved; and after the fall of Gilgalad[4] the lineage of the High-elven Kings was also in Middle-earth only represented by their descendants.

At the end of the First Age the Valar gave to the Half-elven an irrevocable choice to which kindred they would belong. Elrond chose to be of Elven-kind, and became a master of wisdom. To him therefore was granted the same grace as to those of the High Elves that still lingered in Middle-earth: that when weary at last of the mortal lands they could take ship from the Grey Havens and pass into the Uttermost West; and this grace continued after the change of the world. But to the children of Elrond a choice was also appointed: to pass with him from the circles of the world; or if they remained to become mortal and die in Middle-earth. For Elrond, therefore, all chances of the War of the Ring were fraught with sorrow.[5]

---

[1] *The Hobbit*, p. 49; II, p. 133.
[2] II, pp. 24–28.
[3] II, pp. 192–7; IV, pp. 150, 160; VI, pp. 29, 33.
[4] I, pp. 69, 244.
[5] See VI, pp. 108, 112.

Elros chose to be of Man-kind and remain with the Edain; but a great life-span was granted to him many times that of lesser men.

As a reward for their sufferings in the cause against Morgoth, the Valar, the Guardians of the World, granted to the Edain a land to dwell in, removed from the dangers of Middle-earth. Most of them, therefore, set sail over Sea, and guided by the Star of Eärendil came to the great Isle of Elenna, westernmost of all Mortal lands. There they founded the realm of Númenor.

There was a tall mountain in the midst of the land, the Menel-tarma, and from its summit the farsighted could descry the white tower of the Haven of the Eldar in Eressëa. Thence the Eldar came to the Edain and enriched them with knowledge and many gifts; but one command had been laid upon the Númenoreans, the 'Ban of the Valar': they were forbidden to sail west out of sight of their own shores or to attempt to set foot on the Undying Lands. For though a long span of life had been granted to them, in the beginning thrice that of lesser Men, they must remain mortal, since the Valar were not permitted to take from them the Gift of Men (or the Doom of Men, as it was afterwards called).

Elros was the first King of Númenor, and was afterwards known by the High-elven name Tar-Minyatur. His descendants were long-lived but mortal. Later when they became powerful they begrudged the choice of their forefather, desiring the immortality within the life of the world that was the fate of the Eldar, and murmuring against the Ban. In this way began their rebellion which, under the evil teaching of Sauron, brought about the Downfall of Númenor and the ruin of the ancient world, as is told in the *Akallabêth*.

These are the names of the Kings and Queens of Númenor: Elros Tar-Minyatur, Vardamir, Tar-Amandil, Tar-Elendil, Tar-Meneldur, Tar-Aldarion, Tar-Ancalimë (the first Ruling Queen), Tar-Anárion, Tar-Súrion, Tar-Telperiën (the second Queen), Tar-Minastir, Tar-Ciryatan, Tar-Atanamir the Great, Tar-Ancalimon, Tar-Telemmaitë, Tar-Vanimeldë (the third Queen), Tar-Alcarin, Tar-Calmacil.

After Calmacil the Kings took the sceptre in names of the Númenorean (or Adûnaic) tongue: Ar-Adûnakhôr, Ar-Zimrathôn, Ar-Sakalthôr, Ar-Gimilzôr, Ar-Inziladûn. Inziladûn repented of the ways of the Kings and changed his name to Tar-Palantir 'The Farsighted'. His daughter should have been the fourth Queen, Tar-Míriel, but the King's nephew usurped the sceptre and became Ar-Pharazôn the Golden, last King of the Númenoreans.

In the days of Tar-Elendil the first ships of the Númenoreans came back to Middle-earth. His elder child was a daughter, Silmariën. Her son was Valandil, first of the Lords of Andúnië in the west of the land, renowned for their friendship with the Eldar. From him were descended Amandil, the last lord, and his son Elendil the Tall.

The sixth King left only one child, a daughter. She became the first Queen; for it was then made a law of the royal house that the eldest child of the King, whether man or woman, should receive the sceptre.

The realm of Númenor endured to the end of the Second Age and increased ever in power and splendour; and until half the Age had passed the Númenoreans grew also in wisdom and joy. The first sign of the shadow that was to fall upon them appeared in the days of Tar-Minastir, eleventh King. He it was that sent a great force to the aid of Gil-galad. He loved the Eldar but envied them. The Númenoreans had now become great mariners, exploring all the seas eastward, and they began to yearn for the West and the forbidden waters; and the more joyful was their life, the more they began to long for the immortality of the Eldar.

Moreover, after Minastir the Kings became greedy of wealth and power. At first the Númenoreans had come to Middle-earth as teachers and friends of lesser Men afflicted by Sauron; but now their havens became fortresses, holding wide coastlands in subjection. Atanamir and his successors levied heavy tribute, and the ships of the Númenoreans returned laden with spoil.

It was Tar-Atanamir who first spoke openly against the Ban and declared that the life of the Eldar was his by right. Thus the shadow deepened, and the thought of death darkened the hearts of the people. Then the Númenoreans became divided: on the one hand were the Kings and those who followed them, and were estranged from the Eldar and the Valar; on the other were the few who called themselves the Faithful. They lived mostly in the west of the land.

The Kings and their followers little by little abandoned the use of the Eldarin tongues; and at last the twentieth King took his royal name, in Númenorean form, calling himself Ar-Adûnakhôr, 'Lord of the West'. This seemed ill-omened to the Faithful, for hitherto they had given that title only to one of the Valar, or to the Elder King himself.[1] And indeed Ar-Adûnakhôr began to persecute the Faithful and punished those who used the Elven-tongues openly; and the Eldar came no more to Númenor.

The power and wealth of the Númenoreans nonetheless continued to increase; but their years lessened as their fear of death grew, and their joy departed. Tar-Palantir attempted to amend the evil; but it was too late, and there was rebellion and strife in Númenor. When he died, his nephew, leader of the rebellion, seized the sceptre, and became King Ar-Pharazôn. Ar-Pharazôn the Golden was the proudest and most powerful of all the Kings, and no less than the kingship of the world was his desire.

He resolved to challenge Sauron the Great for the supremacy in Middle-earth, and at length he himself set sail with a great navy, and he landed at Umbar. So great was the might and splendour of the Númenoreans that Sauron's own servants deserted him; and Sauron humbled himself, doing homage, and craving pardon. Then Ar-Pharazôn in the folly of his pride carried him back as a prisoner to Númenor. It was not long before he had bewitched the King and was master of his counsel; and soon he had turned the hearts of all the Númenoreans, except the remnant of the Faithful, back towards the darkness.

And Sauron lied to the King, declaring that everlasting life would be his who possessed the Undying Lands, and that the Ban was imposed only to prevent the Kings of Men from surpassing the Valar. 'But great Kings take what is their right,' he said.

[1] II, p. 26.

At length Ar-Pharazôn listened to this counsel, for he felt the waning of his days and was besotted by the fear of Death. He prepared then the greatest armament that the world had seen, and when all was ready he sounded his trumpets and set sail; and he broke the Ban of the Valar, going up with war to wrest everlasting life from the Lords of the West. But when Ar-Pharazôn set foot upon the shores of Aman the Blessed, the Valar laid down their Guardianship and called upon the One, and the world was changed. Númenor was thrown down and swallowed in the Sea, and the Undying Lands were removed for ever from the circles of the world. So ended the glory of Númenor.

The last leaders of the Faithful, Elendil and his sons, escaped from the Downfall with nine ships, bearing a seedling of Nimloth, and the Seven Seeing-stones (gifts of the Eldar to their House);[1] and they were borne on the wind of a great storm and cast upon the shores of Middle-earth. There they established in the North-west the Númenorean realms in exile, Arnor and Gondor.[2] Elendil was the High King and dwelt in the North at Annúminas; and the rule in the South was committed to his sons, Isildur and Anárion. They founded there Osgiliath, between Minas Ithil and Minas Anor,[3] not far from the confines of Mordor. For this good at least they believed had come out of ruin, that Sauron also had perished.

But it was not so. Sauron was indeed caught in the wreck of Númenor, so that the bodily form in which he long had walked perished; but he fled back to Middle-earth, a spirit of hatred borne upon a dark wind. He was unable ever again to assume a form that seemed fair to men, but became black and hideous, and his power thereafter was through terror alone. He re-entered Mordor, and hid there for a time in silence. But his anger was great when he learned that Elendil, whom he most hated, had escaped him, and was now ordering a realm upon his borders.

Therefore, after a time he made war upon the Exiles, before they should take root. Orodruin burst once more into flame, and

[1] III, p. 247; VI, p. 105.
[2] II, p. 36.
[3] II, p. 38.

was named anew in Gondor *Amon Amarth*, Mount Doom. But Sauron struck too soon, before his own power was rebuilt, whereas the power of Gil-galad had increased in his absence; and in the Last Alliance that was made against him Sauron was overthrown and the One Ring was taken from him.[1] So ended the Second Age.

(ii)
THE REALMS IN EXILE

The Northern Line
Heirs of Isildur

Arnor. Elendil †S.A. 3441, Isildur †2, Valandil 249,[2] Eldacar 339, Arantar 435, Tarcil 515, Tarondor 602, Valandur †652, Elendur 777, Eärendur 861.

Arthedain. Amlaith of Fornost[3] (eldest son of Eärendur) 946, Beleg 1029, Mallor 1110, Celepharn 1191, Celebrindor 1272, Malvegil 1349,[4] Argeleb I †1356, Arveleg I 1409, Araphor 1589, Argeleb II 1670, Arvegil 1743, Arveleg II 1813, Araval 1891, Araphant 1964, Arvedui Last-king †1975. End of the North-kingdom.

Chieftains. Aranarth (elder son of Arvedui) 2106, Arahael 2177, Aranuir 2247, Aravir 2319, Aragorn I †2327, Araglas 2455, Arahad I 2523, Aragost 2588, Aravorn 2654, Arahad II 2719, Arassuil 2784, Arathorn I †2848, Argonui 2912, Arador †2930, Arathorn II †2933, Aragorn II F.A. 120.

The Southern Line
Heirs of Anárion

Kings of Gondor. Elendil (Isildur and) Anárion †S.A. 3440,

---

[1] II. p. 37.

[2] He was the fourth son of Isildur, born in Imladris. His brothers were slain in the Gladden Fields.

[3] After Eärendur the Kings no longer took names in High-elven form.

[4] After Malvegil, the Kings at Fornost again claimed lordship over the whole of Arnor, and took names with the prefix *ar* (*a*) in token of this.

Meneldil son of Anárion 158, Cemendur 238, Eärendil 324, Anardil 411, Ostoher 492, Rómendacil I (Tarostar) †541, Turambar 667, Atanatar I 748, Siriondil 830. Here followed the four 'Ship-kings':

Tarannon Falastur 913. He was the first childless king, and was succeeded by the son of his brother Tarciryan. Eärnil I †936, Ciryandil †1015, Hyarmendacil I (Ciryaher) 1149. Gondor now reached the height of its power.

Atanatar II Alcarin 'the Glorious' 1226, Narmacil I 1294. He was the second childless king and was succeeded by his younger brother. Calmacil 1304, Minalcar (regent 1240–1304), crowned as Rómendacil II 1304, died 1366, Valacar. In his time the first disaster of Gondor began, the Kin-strife.

Eldacar son of Valacar (at first called Vinitharya) deposed 1437. Castamir the Usurper †1447. Eldacar restored, died 1490.

Aldamir (second son of Eldacar) †1540. Hyarmendacil II (Vinyarion) 1621, Minardil †1634, Telemnar †1636. Telemnar and all his children perished in the plague; he was succeeded by his nephew, the son of Minastan, second son of Minardil. Tarondor 1798, Telumehtar Umbardacil 1850, Narmacil II †1856, Calimehtar 1936, Ondoher †1944. Ondoher and his two sons were slain in battle. After a year in 1945 the crown was given to the victorious general Eärnil, a descendant of Telumehtar Umbardacil. Eärnil II 2043, Eärnur †2050. Here the line of the Kings came to an end, until it was restored by Elessar Telcontar in 3019. The realm was then ruled by the Stewards.

Stewards of Gondor. The House of Húrin: Pelendur 1998. He ruled for a year after the fall of Ondoher, and advised Gondor to reject Arvedui's claim to the crown. Vorondil the Hunter 2029.[1] Mardil Voronwë 'the Steadfast', the first of the Ruling Stewards. His successors ceased to use High-elven names.

---

[1] See V, p. 16. The wild-kine that were still to be found near the Sea of Rhûn were said in legend to be descended from the Kine of Araw, the huntsman of the Valar, who alone of the Valar came often to Middle-earth in the Elder Days. *Oromë* is the High-elven form of his name (V, p. 125).

Ruling Stewards. Mardil 2080, Eradan 2116, Herion 2148, Beleg-
orn 2204, Húrin I 2244, Túrin I 2278, Hador 2395, Barahir
2412, Dior 2435, Denethor I 2477, Boromir 2489, Cirion
2567. In his time the Rohirrim came to Calenardhon.

Hallas 2605, Húrin II 2628, Belecthor I 2655, Orodreth
2685, Ecthelion I 2698, Egalmoth 2743, Beren 2763, Beregond
2811, Belecthor II 2872, Thorondir 2882, Túrin II 2914, Turgon 2953, Ecthelion II 2984, Denethor II. He was the last of
the Ruling Stewards, and was followed by his second son
Faramir, Lord of Emyn Arnen, Steward to King Elessar, F.A.
82.

(iii)
ERIADOR, ARNOR, AND
THE HEIRS OF·ISILDUR

'Eriador was of old the name of all the lands between the Misty
Mountains and the Blue; in the South it was bounded by the
Greyflood and the Glanduin that flows into it above Tharbad.

'At its greatest Arnor included all Eriador, except the regions
beyond the Lune, and the lands east of Greyflood and Loudwater, in which lay Rivendell and Hollin. Beyond the Lune was
Elvish country, green and quiet, where no Men went; but
Dwarves dwelt, and still dwell, in the east side of the Blue Mountains, especially in those parts south of the Gulf of Lune, where
they have mines that are still in use. For this reason they were
accustomed to pass east along the Great Road, as they had done
for long years before we came to the Shire. At the Grey Havens
dwelt Círdan the Shipwright, and some say he dwells there still,
until the Last Ship sets sail into the West. In the days of the
Kings most of the High Elves that still lingered in Middle-earth
dwelt with Círdan or in the seaward lands of Lindon. If any now
remain they are few.'

The North-kingdom and the Dúnedain

After Elendil and Isildur there were eight High Kings of Arnor.
After Eärendur, owing to dissensions among his sons their realm
was divided into three: Arthedain, Rhudaur, and Cardolan.

Arthedain was in the North-west and included the land between Brandywine and Lune, and also the land north of the Great Road as far as the Weather Hills. Rhudaur was in the North-east and lay between the Ettenmoors, the Weather Hills, and the Misty Mountains, but included also the Angle between the Hoarwell and the Loudwater. Cardolan was in the South, its bounds being the Brandywine, the Greyflood, and the Great Road.

In Arthedain the line of Isildur was maintained and endured, but the line soon perished in Cardolan and Rhudaur. There was often strife between the kingdoms, which hastened the waning of the Dúnedain. The chief matter of debate was the possession of the Weather Hills and the land westward towards Bree. Both Rhudaur and Cardolan desired to possess Amon Sûl (Weathertop), which stood on the borders of their realms; for the Tower of Amon Sûl held the chief *Palantír* of the North, and the other two were both in the keeping of Arthedain.

'It was in the beginning of the reign of Malvegil of Arthedain that evil came to Arnor. For at that time the realm of Angmar arose in the North beyond the Ettenmoors. Its lands lay on both sides of the Mountains, and there were gathered many evil men, and Orcs, and other fell creatures. [The lord of that land was known as the Witch-king, but it was not known until later that he was indeed the chief of the Ringwraiths, who came north with the purpose of destroying the Dúnedain in Arnor, seeing hope in their disunion, while Gondor was strong.]'

In the days of Argeleb son of Malvegil, since no descendants of Isildur remained in the other kingdoms, the kings of Arthedain again claimed the lordship of all Arnor. The claim was resisted by Rhudaur. There the Dúnedain were few, and power had been seized by an evil lord of the Hillmen, who was in secret league with Angmar. Argeleb therefore fortified the Weather Hills;[1] but he was slain in battle with Rhudaur and Angmar.

Arveleg son of Argeleb, with the help of Cardolan and Lindon, drove back his enemies from the Hills; and for many years Arthedain and Cardolan held in force a frontier along the

[1] I, p. 244.

Weather Hills, the Great Road, and the lower Hoarwell. It is said that at this time Rivendell was besieged.

A great host came out of Angmar in 1409, and crossing the river entered Cardolan and surrounded Weathertop. The Dúnedain were defeated and Arveleg was slain. The Tower of Amon Sûl was burned and razed; but the *palantír* was saved and carried back in retreat to Fornost, Rhudaur was occupied by evil Men subject to Angmar,[1] and the Dúnedain that remained there were slain or fled west. Cardolan was ravaged. Araphor son of Arveleg was not yet full-grown, but he was valiant, and with aid from Círdan he repelled the enemy from Fornost and the North Downs. A remnant of the faithful among the Dúnedain of Cardolan also held out in Tyrn Gorthad (the Barrowdowns), or took refuge in the Forest behind.

It is said that Angmar was for a time subdued by the Elvenfolk coming from Lindon; and from Rivendell, for Elrond brought help over the Mountains out of Lórien. It was at this time that the Stoors that had dwelt in the Angle (between Hoarwell and Loudwater) fled west and south, because of the wars, and the dread of Angmar, and because the land and clime of Eriador, especially in the east, worsened and became unfriendly. Some returned to Wilderland, and dwelt beside the Gladden, becoming a riverside people of fishers.

In the days of Argeleb II the plague came into Eriador from the South-east, and most of the people of Cardolan perished, especially in Minhiriath. The Hobbits and all other peoples suffered greatly, but the plague lessened as it passed northwards, and the northern parts of Arthedain were little affected. It was at this time that an end came of the Dúnedain of Cardolan, and evil spirits out of Angmar and Rhudaur entered into the deserted mounds and dwelt there.

'It is said that the mounds of Tyrn Gorthad, as the Barrow-downs were called of old, are very ancient, and that many were built in the days of the old world of the First Age by the forefathers of the Edain, before they crossed the Blue Mountains into Beleriand, of which Lindon is all that now remains. Those

---

[1] I, p. 265.

hills were therefore revered by the Dúnedain after their return; and there many of their lords and kings were buried. [Some say that the mound in which the Ring-bearer was imprisoned had been the grave of the last prince of Cardolan, who fell in the war of 1409.]'

'In 1974 the power of Angmar arose again, and the Witch-king came down upon Arthedain before winter was ended. He captured Fornost, and drove most of the remaining Dúnedain over the Lune; among them were the sons of the king. But King Arvedui held out upon the North Downs until the last, and then fled north with some of his guard; and they escaped by the swiftness of their horses.

'For a while Arvedui hid in the tunnels of the old dwarf-mines near the far end of the Mountains, but he was driven at last by hunger to seek the help of the Lossoth, the Snowmen of Forochel.[1] Some of these he found in camp by the seashore; but they did not help the king willingly, for he had nothing to offer them, save a few jewels which they did not value; and they were afraid of the Witch-king, who (they said) could make frost or thaw at his will. But partly out of pity for the gaunt king and his men, and partly out of fear of their weapons, they gave them a little food and built for them snow-huts. There Arvedui was forced to wait, hoping for help from the south; for his horses had perished.

'When Círdan heard from Aranarth son of Arvedui of the king's flight to the north, he at once sent a ship to Forochel to seek for him. The ship came there at last after many days, because of contrary winds, and the mariners saw from afar the

---

[1] These are a strange, unfriendly people, remnant of the Forodwaith, Men of far-off days, accustomed to the bitter colds of the realm of Morgoth. Indeed those colds linger still in that region, though they lie hardly more than a hundred leagues north of the Shire. The Lossoth house in the snow, and it is said that they can run on the ice with bones on their feet, and have carts without wheels. They live mostly, inaccessible to their enemies, on the great Cape of Forochel that shuts off to the north-west the immense bay of that name; but they often camp on the south shores of the bay at the feet of the Mountains.

little fire of drift-wood which the lost men contrived to keep alight. But the winter was long in loosing its grip that year; and though it was then March, the ice was only beginning to break, and lay far out from the shore.

'When the Snowmen saw the ship they were amazed and afraid, for they had seen no such ship on the sea within their memories; but they had become now more friendly, and they drew the king and those that survived of his company out over the ice in their sliding carts, as far as they dared. In this way a boat from the ship was able to reach them.

'But the Snowmen were uneasy: for they said that they smelled danger in the wind. And the chief of the Lossoth said to Arvedui: "Do not mount on this sea-monster! If they have them, let the seamen bring us food and other things that we need, and you may stay here till the Witch-king goes home. For in summer his power wanes; but now his breath is deadly, and his cold arm is long."

'But Arvedui did not take his counsel. He thanked him, and at parting gave him his ring, saying: "This is a thing of worth beyond your reckoning. For its ancientry alone. It has no power, save the esteem in which those hold it who love my house. It will not help you, but if ever you are in need, my kin will ransom it with great store of all that you desire."[1]

'Yet the counsel of the Lossoth was good, by chance or by foresight; for the ship had not reached the open sea when a great storm of wind arose, and came with blinding snow out of the North; and it drove the ship back upon the ice and piled ice up against it. Even the mariners of Círdan were helpless, and in the night the ice crushed the hull, and the ship foundered. So perished Arvedui Last-king, and with him the *palantíri* were buried in the sea.[2] It was long afterwards that news of the shipwreck of Forochel was learned from the Snowmen.'

[1] In this way the ring of the House of Isildur was saved; for it was afterwards ransomed by the Dúnedain. It is said that it was none other than the ring which Felagund of Nargothrond gave to Barahir, and Beren recovered at great peril.

[2] These were the Stones of Annúminas and Amon Sûl. The only Stone left in the North was the one in the Tower on Emyn Beraid that looks towards the Gulf of Lune. That was guarded by the Elves, and though we never knew it, it remained there, until Círdan put it aboard Elrond's ship when he left (I, pp. 59, 143). But we are told that it was

The Shire-folk survived, though war swept over them and most of them fled into hiding. To the help of the king they sent some archers who never returned; and others went also to the battle in which Angmar was overthrown (of which more is said in the annals of the South). Afterwards in the peace that followed the Shire-folk ruled themselves and prospered. They chose a Thain to take the place of the King, and were content; though for a long time many still looked for the return of the King. But at last that hope was forgotten, and remained only in the saying *When the King comes back*, used of some good that could not be achieved, or of some evil that could not be amended. The first Shire-thain was one Bucca of the Marish, from whom the Old-bucks claimed descent. He became Thain in 379 of our reckoning (1979).

After Arvedui the North-kingdom ended, for the Dúnedain were now few and all the peoples of Eriador diminished. Yet the line of the kings was continued by the Chieftains of the Dúnedain, of whom Aranarth son of Arvedui was the first. Arahael his son was fostered in Rivendell, and so were all the sons of the chief-tains after him; and there also were kept the heirlooms of their house: the ring of Barahir, the shards of Narsil, the star of Elendil, and the sceptre of Annúminas.[1]

---

unlike the others and not in accord with them; it looked only to the Sea. Elendil set it there so that he could look back with 'straight sight' and see Eressëa in the vanished West; but the bent seas below covered Númenor for ever.

[1] The sceptre was the chief mark of royalty in Númenor, the King tells us; and that was also so in Arnor, whose kings wore no crown, but bore a single white gem, the Elendilmir, Star of Elendil, bound on their brows with a silver fillet (I, p. 193; V, pp. 138, 155; VI, p.99). In speaking of a crown (I, p. 224; II, p. 42) Bilbo no doubt referred to Gondor; he seems to have become well acquainted with matters concerning Ara-gorn's line. The sceptre of Númenor is said to have perished with Ar-Pharazôn. That of Annúminas was the silver rod of the Lords of Andúnië, and is now perhaps the most ancient work of Men's hands preserved in Middle-earth. It was already more than five thousand years old when Elrond surrendered it to Aragorn (VI, p. 106). The crown of Gondor was derived from the form of a Númenorean war-helm. In the beginning it was indeed a plain helm; and it is said to have been the one that Isildur wore in the Battle of Dagorlad (for the helm of Anárion was

'When the kingdom ended the Dúnedain passed into the shadows and became a secret and wandering people, and their deeds and labours were seldom sung or recorded. Little now is remembered of them since Elrond departed. Although even before the Watchful Peace ended evil things again began to attack Eriador or to invade it secretly, the Chieftains for the most part lived out their long lives. Aragorn I, it is said, was slain by wolves, which ever after remained a peril in Eriador, and are not yet ended. In the days of Arahad I the Orcs, who had, as later appeared, long been secretly occupying strongholds in the Misty Mountains, so as to bar all the passes into Eriador, suddenly revealed themselves. In 2509 Celebrían wife of Elrond was journeying to Lórien when she was waylaid in the Redhorn Pass, and her escort being scattered by the sudden assault of the Orcs, she was seized and carried off. She was pursued and rescued by Elladan and Elrohir, but not before she had suffered torment and had received a poisoned wound.[1] She was brought back to Imladris, and though healed in body by Elrond, lost all delight in Middle-earth, and the next year went to the Havens and passed over Sea. And later in the days of Arassuil, Orcs, multiplying again in the Misty Mountains, began to ravage the lands, and the Dúnedain and the sons of Elrond fought with them. It was at this time that a large band came so far west as to enter the Shire, and were driven off by Bandobras Took.[2]

There were fifteen Chieftains, before the sixteenth and last was born, Aragorn II, who became again King of both Gondor and Arnor. 'Our King, we call him; and when he comes north to his house in Annúminas restored and stays for a while by Lake Evendim, then everyone in the Shire is glad. But he does not enter this land and binds himself by the law that he has made, that none of the Big People shall pass its borders. But he rides often with many fair people to the Great Bridge, and there he welcomes his friends, and any others who wish to see him;

---

crushed by the stone-cast from Barad-dûr that slew him). But in the days of Atanatar Alcarin this was replaced by the jewelled helm that was used in the crowning of Aragorn.

[1] II, p. 16.
[2] I, p. 7; VI, p. 161.

and some ride away with him and stay in his house as long as they have a mind. Thain Peregrin has been there many times; and so has Master Samwise the Mayor. His daughter Elanor the Fair is one of the maids of Queen Evenstar.'

It was the pride and wonder of the Northern Line that, though their power departed and their people dwindled, through all the many generations the succession was unbroken from father to son. Also, though the length of lives of the Dúnedain grew ever less in Middle-earth, after the ending of their kings the waning was swifter in Gondor; and many of the Chieftains of the North still lived to twice the age of Men, and far beyond the days of even the oldest amongst us. Aragorn indeed lived to be two hundred and ten years old, longer than any of his line since King Arvegil; but in Aragorn Elessar the dignity of the kings of old was renewed.

(iv)
GONDOR AND THE HEIRS OF ANÁRION

There were thirty-one kings in Gondor after Anárion who was slain before the Barad-dûr. Though war never ceased on their borders, for more than a thousand years the Dúnedain of the South grew in wealth and power by land and sea, until the reign of Atanatar II, who was called Alcarin, the Glorious. Yet the signs of decay had then already appeared; for the high men of the South married late, and their children were few. The first childless king was Falastur, and the second Narmacil I, the son of Atanatar Alcarin.

It was Ostoher the seventh king who rebuilt Minas Anor, where afterwards the kings dwelt in summer rather than in Osgiliath. In his time Gondor was first attacked by wild men out of the East. But Tarostar, his son, defeated them and drove them out, and took the name of Rómendacil 'East-victor'. He was, however, later slain in battle with fresh hordes of Easterlings. Turambar his son avenged him, and won much territory eastwards.

With Tarannon, the twelfth king, began the line of the Ship-kings, who built navies and extended the sway of Gondor along the coasts west and south of the Mouths of Anduin. To commemorate his victories as Captain of the Hosts, Tarannon took the crown in the name of Falastur 'Lord of the Coasts'.

Eärnil I, his nephew, who succeeded him, repaired the ancient haven of Pelargir, and built a great navy. He laid siege by sea and land to Umbar, and took it, and it became a great harbour and fortress of the power of Gondor.[1] But Eärnil did not long survive his triumph. He was lost with many ships and men in a great storm off Umbar. Ciryandil his son continued the building of ships; but the Men of the Harad, led by the lords that had been driven from Umbar, came up with great power against that stronghold, and Ciryandil fell in battle in Haradwaith.

For many years Umbar was invested, but could not be taken because of the sea-power of Gondor. Ciryaher son of Ciryandil bided his time, and at last when he had gathered strength he came down from the north by sea and by land, and crossing the River Harnen his armies utterly defeated the Men of the Harad, and their kings were compelled to acknowledge the overlordship of Gondor (1050). Ciryaher then took the name of Hyarmendacil 'South-victor'.

The might of Hyarmendacil no enemy dared to contest during the remainder of his long reign. He was king for one hundred and thirty-four years, the longest reign but one of all the Line of Anárion. In his day Gondor reached the summit of its power. The realm then extended north to Celebrant and the southern eaves of Mirkwood; west to the Greyflood; east to the inland Sea of Rhûn; south to the River Harnen, and thence along the coast to the peninsula and haven of Umbar. The Men of the Vales of Anduin acknowledged its authority; and the kings of the Harad did homage to Gondor, and their sons lived as hostages in the court of its King. Mordor was desolate, but was watched over by great fortresses that guarded the passes.

---

[1] The great cape and land-locked firth of Umbar had been Númenorean land since days of old; but it was a stronghold of the King's Men, who were afterwards called the Black Númenoreans, corrupted by Sauron, and who hated above all the followers of Elendil. After the fall of Sauron their race swiftly dwindled or became merged with the Men of Middle-earth, but they inherited without lessening their hatred of Gondor. Umbar, therefore, was only taken at great cost.

So ended the line of the Ship-kings. Atanatar Alcarin son of Hyarmendacil lived in great splendour, so that men said *precious stones are pebbles in Gondor for children to play with*. But Atanatar loved ease and did nothing to maintain the power that he had inherited, and his two sons were of like temper. The waning of Gondor had already begun before he died, and was doubtless observed by its enemies. The watch upon Mordor was neglected. Nonetheless it was not until the days of Valacar that the first great evil came upon Gondor: the civil war of the Kin-strife, in which great loss and ruin was caused and never fully repaired.

Minalcar, son of Calmacil, was a man of great vigour, and in 1240 Narmacil, to rid himself of all cares, made him Regent of the realm. From that time onwards he governed Gondor in the name of the kings until he succeeded his father. His chief concern was with the Northmen.

These had increased greatly in the peace brought by the power of Gondor. The kings showed them favour, since they were the nearest in kin of lesser Men to the Dúnedain (being for the most part descendants of those peoples from whom the Edain of old had come); and they gave them wide lands beyond Anduin south of Greenwood the Great, to be a defence against men of the East. For in the past the attacks of the Easterlings had come mostly over the plain between the Inland Sea and the Ash Mountains.

In the days of Narmacil I their attacks began again, though at first with little force; but it was learned by the regent that the Northmen did not always remain true to Gondor, and some would join forces with the Easterlings, either out of greed for spoil, or in the furtherance of feuds among their princes. Minalcar therefore in 1248 led out a great force, and between Rhovanion and the Inland Sea he defeated a large army of the Easterlings and destroyed all their camps and settlements east of the Sea. He then took the name of Rómendacil.

On his return Rómendacil fortified the west shore of Anduin as far as the inflow of the Limlight, and forbade any stranger to pass down the River beyond the Emyn Muil. He it was that built the pillars of the Argonath at the entrance to Nen Hithoel. But since he needed men, and desired to strengthen the bond between Gondor and the Northmen, he took many of them into his service and gave to some high rank in his armies.

Rómendacil showed especial favour to Vidugavia, who had aided him in the war. He called himself King of Rhovanion, and was indeed the most powerful of the Northern princes, though his own realm lay between Greenwood and the River Celduin.[1] In 1250 Rómendacil sent his son Valacar as an ambassador to dwell for a while with Vidugavia and make himself acquainted with the language, manners, and policies of the Northmen. But Valacar far exceeded his father's designs. He grew to love the Northern lands and people, and he married Vidumavi, daughter of Vidugavia. It was some years before he returned. From this marriage came later the war of the Kin-strife.

'For the high men of Gondor already looked askance at the Northmen among them; and it was a thing unheard of before that the heir of the crown, or any son of the King, should wed one of lesser and alien race. There was already rebellion in the southern provinces when King Valacar grew old. His queen had been a fair and noble lady, but short-lived according to the fate of lesser Men, and the Dúnedain feared that her descendants would prove the same and fall from the majesty of the Kings of Men. Also they were unwilling to accept as lord her son, who though he was now called Eldacar, had been born in an alien country and was named in his youth Vinitharya, a name of his mother's people.

'Therefore when Eldacar succeeded his father there was war in Gondor. But Eldacar did not prove easy to thrust from his heritage. To the lineage of Gondor he added the fearless spirit of the Northmen. He was handsome and valiant, and showed no sign of ageing more swiftly than his father. When the confederates led by descendants of the kings rose against him, he opposed them to the end of his strength. At last he was besieged in Osgiliath, and held it long, until hunger and the greater forces of the rebels drove him out, leaving the city in flames. In that siege and burning the Dome of Osgiliath was destroyed, and the *palantír* was lost in the waters.

'But Eldacar eluded his enemies, and came to the North, to

---

[1] The River Running.

his kinsfolk in Rhovanion. Many gathered to him there, both of the Northmen in the service of Gondor, and of the Dúnedain of the northern parts of the realm. For many of the latter had learned to esteem him, and many more came to hate his usurper. This was Castamir, grandson of Calimehtar, younger brother of Rómendacil II. He was not only one of those nearest by blood to the crown, but he had the greatest following of all the rebels; for he was the Captain of Ships, and was supported by the people of the coasts and of the great havens of Pelargir and Umbar.

'Castamir had not long sat upon the throne before he proved himself haughty and ungenerous. He was a cruel man, as he had first shown in the taking of Osgiliath. He caused Ornendil son of Eldacar, who was captured, to be put to death; and the slaughter and destruction done in the city at his bidding far exceeded the needs of war. This was remembered in Minas Anor and in Ithilien; and there love for Castamir was further lessened when it became seen that he cared little for the land, and thought only of the fleets, and purposed to remove the king's seat to Pelargir.

'Thus he had been king only ten years, when Eldacar, seeing his time, came with a great army out of the north, and folk flocked to him from Calenardhon and Anórien and Ithilien. There was a great battle in Lebennin at the Crossings of Erui, in which much of the best blood in Gondor was shed. Eldacar himself slew Castamir in combat, and so was avenged for Ornendil; but Castamir's sons escaped, and with others of their kin and many people of the fleets they held out long at Pelargir.

'When they had gathered there all the force that they could (for Eldacar had no ships to beset them by sea) they sailed away, and established themselves at Umbar. There they made a refuge for all the enemies of the king, and a lordship independent of his crown. Umbar remained at war with Gondor for many lives of men, a threat to its coastlands and to all traffic on the sea. It was never again completely subdued until the days of Elessar; and the region of South Gondor became a debatable land between the Corsairs and the Kings.'

'The loss of Umbar was grievous to Gondor, not only because the realm was diminished in the south and its hold upon the

Men of the Harad was loosened, but because it was there that Ar-Pharazôn the Golden, last King of Númenor, had landed and humbled the might of Sauron. Though great evil had come after, even the followers of Elendil remembered with pride the coming of the great host of Ar-Pharazôn out of the deeps of the Sea; and on the highest hill of the headland above the Haven they had set a great white pillar as a monument. It was crowned with a globe of crystal that took the rays of the Sun and of the Moon and shone like a bright star that could be seen in clear weather even on the coasts of Gondor or far out upon the western sea. So it stood, until after the second arising of Sauron, which now approached, Umbar fell under the domination of his servants, and the memorial of his humiliation was thrown down.'

After the return of Eldacar the blood of the kingly house and other houses of the Dúnedain became more mingled with that of lesser Men. For many of the great had been slain in the Kin-strife; while Eldacar showed favour to the Northmen, by whose help he had regained the crown, and the people of Gondor were replenished by great numbers that came from Rhovanion.

This mingling did not at first hasten the waning of the Dúnedain, as had been feared; but the waning still proceeded, little by little, as it had before. For no doubt it was due above all to Middle-earth itself, and to the slow withdrawing of the gifts of the Númenoreans after the downfall of the Land of the Star. Eldacar lived to his two hundred and thirty-fifth year, and was king for fifty-eight years, of which ten were spent in exile.

The second and greatest evil came upon Gondor in the reign of Telemnar, the twenty-sixth king, whose father Minardil, son of Eldacar, was slain at Pelargir by the Corsairs of Umbar. (They were led by Angamaitë and Sangahyando, the great-grandsons of Castamir.) Soon after a deadly plague came with dark winds out of the East. The King and all his children died, and great numbers of the people of Gondor, especially those that lived in Osgiliath. Then for weariness and fewness of men the watch on the borders of Mordor ceased and the fortresses that guarded the passes were unmanned.

Later it was noted that these things happened even as the

Shadow grew deep in Greenwood, and many evil things re-appeared, signs of the arising of Sauron. It is true that the enemies of Gondor also suffered, or they might have over-whelmed it in its weakness; but Sauron could wait, and it may well be that the opening of Mordor was what he chiefly desired.

When King Telemnar died the White Trees of Minas Anor also withered and died. But Tarondor, his nephew, who suc-ceeded him, replanted a seedling in the citadel. He it was who removed the King's house permanently to Minas Anor, for Osgiliath was now partly deserted, and began to fall into ruin. Few of those who had fled from the plague into Ithilien or to the western dales were willing to return.

Tarondor, coming young to the throne, had the longest reign of all the Kings of Gondor; but he could achieve little more than the reordering of his realm within, and the slow nursing of its strength. But Telumehtar his son, remembering the death of Minardil, and being troubled by the insolence of the Corsairs, who raided his coasts even as far as the Anfalas, gathered his forces and in 1810 took Umbar by storm. In that war the last descendants of Castamir perished, and Umbar was again held for a while by the kings. Telumehtar added to his name the title Umbardacil. But in the new evils that soon befell Gondor Umbar was again lost, and fell into the hands of the Men of the Harad.

The third evil was the invasion of the Wainriders, which sapped the waning strength of Gondor in wars that lasted for almost a hundred years. The Wainriders were a people, or a confederacy of many peoples, that came from the East; but they were stronger and better armed than any that had appeared before. They jour-neyed in great wains, and their chieftains fought in chariots. Stirred up, as was afterwards seen, by the emissaries of Sauron, they made a sudden assault upon Gondor, and King Narmacil II was slain in battle with them beyond Anduin in 1856. The people of eastern and southern Rhovanion were enslaved; and the frontiers of Gondor were for that time withdrawn to the Anduin and the Emyn Muil. [At this time it is thought that the Ringwraiths re-entered Mordor.]

Calimehtar, son of Narmacil II, helped by a revolt in Rhov-anion, avenged his father with a great victory over the Easterlings upon Dagorlad in 1899, and for a while the peril was averted. It was in the reign of Araphant in the North and of Ondoher son of Calimehtar in the South that the two kingdoms again took counsel together after long silence and estrangement. For at last they perceived that some single power and will was directing the assault from many quarters upon the survivors of Númenor. It was at that time that Arvedui heir of Araphant wedded Fíriel daughter of Ondoher (1940). But neither kingdom was able to send help to the other; for Angmar renewed its attack upon Arthedain at the same time as the Wainriders reappeared in great force.

Many of the Wainriders now passed south of Mordor and made alliance with men of Khand and of Near Harad; and in this great assault from north and south, Gondor came near to destruction. In 1944 King Ondoher and both his sons, Artamir and Faramir, fell in battle north of the Morannon, and the enemy poured into Ithilien. But Eärnil, Captain of the Southern Army, won a great victory in South Ithilien and destroyed the army of Harad that had crossed the River Poros. Hastening north, he gathered to him all that he could of the retreating Northern Army and came up against the main camp of the Wainriders, while they were feasting and revelling, believing that Gondor was overthrown and that nothing remained but to take the spoil. Eärnil stormed the camp and set fire to the wains, and drove the enemy in a great rout out of Ithilien. A great part of those who fled before him perished in the Dead Marshes.

'On the death of Ondoher and his sons, Arvedui of the North-kingdom claimed the crown of Gondor, as the direct descendant of Isildur, and as the husband of Fíriel, only surviving child of Ondoher. The claim was rejected. In this Pelendur, the Steward of King Ondoher, played the chief part.

'The Council of Gondor answered: "The crown and royalty of Gondor belongs solely to the heirs of Meneldil, son of Anárion, to whom Isildur relinquished this realm. In Gondor this heritage is reckoned through the sons only; and we have not heard that the law is otherwise in Arnor."

'To this Arvedui replied: "Elendil had two sons, of whom Isildur was the elder and the heir of his father. We have heard

that the name of Elendil stands to this day at the head of the
line of the Kings of Gondor, since he was accounted the high
king of all lands of the Dúnedain. While Elendil still lived, the
conjoint rule in the South was committed to his sons; but when
Elendil fell, Isildur departed to take up the high kingship of his
father, and committed the rule in the South in like manner to
the son of his brother. He did not relinquish his royalty in
Gondor, nor intend that the realm of Elendil should be divided
for ever.

' "Moreover, in Númenor of old the sceptre descended to the
eldest child of the king, whether man or woman. It is true that
the law has not been observed in the lands of exile ever troubled
by war; but such was the law of our people, to which we now
refer, seeing that the sons of Ondoher died childless."[1]

'To this Gondor made no answer. The crown was claimed
by Eärnil, the victorious captain; and it was granted to him with
the approval of all the Dúnedain in Gondor, since he was of the
royal house. He was the son of Siriondil, son of Calimmacil, son
of Arciryas brother of Narmacil II. Arvedui did not press his
claim; for he had neither the power nor the will to oppose the
choice of the Dúnedain of Gondor; yet the claim was never
forgotten by his descendants even when their kingship had
passed away. For the time was now drawing near when the
North-kingdom would come to an end.

'Arvedui was indeed the last king, as his name signifies. It is
said that this name was given to him at his birth by Malbeth the
Seer, who said to his father: "*Arvedui* you shall call him, for he
will be the last in Arthedain. Though a choice will come to the
Dúnedain, and if they take the one that seems less hopeful, then
your son will change his name and become king of a great realm.
If not, then much sorrow and many lives of men shall pass, until
the Dúnedain arise and are united again."

[1] That law was made in Númenor (as we have learned from the
King) when Tar-Aldarion, the sixth king, left only one child, a daughter.
She became the first Ruling Queen, Tar-Ancalimë. But the law was
otherwise before her time. Tar-Elendil, the fourth king, was succeeded
by his son Tar-Meneldur, though his daughter Silmariën was the elder.
It was, however, from Silmariën that Elendil was descended.

'In Gondor also one king only followed Eärnil. It may be that if the crown and the sceptre had been united, then the kingship would have been maintained and much evil averted. But Eärnil was a wise man, and not arrogant, even if, as to most men in Gondor, the realm in Arthedain seemed a small thing, for all the lineage of its lords.

'He sent messages to Arvedui announcing that he received the crown of Gondor, according to the laws and the needs of the South-kingdom, "but I do not forget the royalty of Arnor, nor deny our kinship, nor wish that the realms of Elendil should be estranged. I will send to your aid when you have need, so far as I am able."

'It was, however, long before Eärnil felt himself sufficiently secure to do as he promised. King Araphant continued with dwindling strength to hold off the assaults of Angmar, and Arvedui when he succeeded did likewise; but at last in the autumn of 1973 messages came to Gondor that Arthedain was in great straits, and that the Witch-king was preparing a last stroke against it. Then Eärnil sent his son Eärnur north with a fleet, as swiftly as he could, and with as great strength as he could spare. Too late. Before Eärnur reached the havens of Lindon, the Witch-king had conquered Arthedain and Arvedui had perished.

'But when Eärnur came to the Grey Havens there was joy and great wonder among both Elves and Men. So great in draught and so many were his ships that they could scarcely find harbourage, though both the Harlond and the Forlond also were filled; and from them descended an army of power, with munition and provision for a war of great kings. Or so it seemed to the people of the North, though this was but a small sending-force of the whole might of Gondor. Most of all, the horses were praised, for many of them came from the Vales of Anduin and with them were riders tall and fair, and proud princes of Rhovanion.

'Then Círdan summoned all who would come to him, from Lindon or Arnor, and when all was ready the host crossed the Lune and marched north to challenge the Witch-king of Angmar. He was now dwelling, it is said, in Fornost, which he had filled with evil folk, usurping the house and rule of the kings. In his pride he did not await the onset of his enemies in his stronghold, but went out to meet them, thinking to sweep them, as others before, into the Lune.

'But the Host of the West came down on him out of the Hills of Evendim, and there was a great battle on the plain between Nenuial and the North Downs. The forces of Angmar were already giving way and retreating towards Fornost when the main body of the horsemen that had passed round the hills came down from the north and scattered them in a great rout. Then the Witch-king, with all that he could gather from the wreck, fled northwards, seeking his own land of Angmar. Before he could gain the shelter of Carn Dûm the cavalry of Gondor overtook him with Eärnur riding at their head. At the same time a force under Glorfindel the Elf-lord came up out of Rivendell. Then so utterly was Angmar defeated that not a man nor an orc of that realm remained west of the Mountains.

'But it is said that when all was lost suddenly the Witch-king himself appeared, black-robed and black-masked upon a black horse. Fear fell upon all who beheld him; but he singled out the Captain of Gondor for the fullness of his hatred, and with a terrible cry he rode straight upon him. Eärnur would have withstood him; but his horse could not endure that onset, and it swerved and bore him far away before he could master it.

'Then the Witch-king laughed, and none that heard it ever forgot the horror of that cry. But Glorfindel rode up then on his white horse, and in the midst of his laughter the Witch-king turned to flight and passed into the shadows. For night came down on the battlefield, and he was lost, and none saw whither he went.

'Eärnur now rode back, but Glorfindel, looking into the gathering dark, said: "Do not pursue him! He will not return to this land. Far off yet is his doom, and not by the hand of man will he fall." These words many remembered; but Eärnur was angry, desiring only to be avenged for his disgrace.

'So ended the evil realm of Angmar; and so did Eärnur, Captain of Gondor, earn the chief hatred of the Witch-king; but many years were still to pass before that was revealed.'

★　　★　　★

It was thus in the reign of King Eärnil, as later became clear, that the Witch-king escaping from the North came to Mordor, and there gathered the other Ringwraiths, of whom he was the chief. But it was not until 2000 that they issued from Mordor by the Pass of Cirith Ungol and laid siege to Minas Ithil. This they took in 2002, and captured the *palantír* of the tower. They ·were not expelled while the Third Age lasted; and Minas Ithil became a place of fear, and was renamed Minas Morgul. Many of the people that still remained in Ithilien deserted it.

'Eärnur was a man like his father in valour, but not in wisdom. He was a man of strong body and hot mood; but he would take no wife, for his only pleasure was in fighting, or in the exercise of arms. His prowess was such that none in Gondor could stand against him in those weapon-sports in which he delighted, seeming rather a champion than a captain or king, and retaining his vigour and skill to a later age than was then usual.'

When Eärnur received the crown in 2043 the King of Minas Morgul challenged him to single combat, taunting him that he had not dared to stand before him in battle in the North. For that time Mardil the Steward restrained the wrath of the king. Minas Anor, which had become the chief city of the realm since the days of King Telemnar, and the residence of the kings, was now renamed Minas Tirith, as the city ever on guard against the evil of Morgul.

Eärnur had held the crown only seven years when the Lord of Morgul repeated his challenge, taunting the king that to the faint heart of his youth he had now added the weakness of age. Then Mardil could no longer restrain him, and he rode with a small escort of knights to the gate of Minas Morgul. None of that riding were ever heard of again. It was believed in Gondor that the faithless enemy had trapped the king, and that he had died in torment in Minas Morgul; but since there were no witnesses of his death, Mardil the Good Steward ruled Gondor in his name for many years.

Now the descendants of the kings had become few. Their numbers had been greatly diminished in the Kin-strife; whereas since that time the kings had become jealous and watchful of those near akin. Often those on whom suspicion fell had fled to

Umbar and there joined the rebels; while others had renounced their lineage and taken wives not of Númenorean blood.

So it was that no claimant to the crown could be found who was of pure blood, or whose claim all would allow; and all feared the memory of the Kin-strife, knowing that if any such dissension arose again, then Gondor would perish. Therefore, though the years lengthened, the Steward continued to rule Gondor, and the crown of Elendil lay in the lap of King Eärnil in the Houses of the Dead, where Eärnur had left it.

The Stewards

The House of the Stewards was called the House of Húrin, for they were descendants of the Steward of King Minardil (1621–34), Húrin of Emyn Arnen, a man of high Númenorean race. After his day the kings had always chosen their stewards from among his descendants; and after the days of Pelendur the Stewardship became hereditary as a kingship, from father to son or nearest kin.

Each new Steward indeed took office with the oath 'to hold rod and rule in the name of the king, until he shall return'. But these soon became words of ritual little heeded, for the Stewards exercised all the power of the kings. Yet many in Gondor still believed that a king would indeed return in some time to come; and some remembered the ancient line of the North, which it was rumoured still lived on in the shadows. But against such thoughts the Ruling Stewards hardened their hearts.

Nonetheless the Stewards never sat on the ancient throne; and they wore no crown, and held no sceptre. They bore a white rod only as the token of their office; and their banner was white without charge; but the royal banner had been sable, upon which was displayed a white tree in blossom beneath seven stars.

After Mardil Voronwë, who was reckoned the first of the line, there followed twenty-four Ruling Stewards of Gondor, until the time of Denethor II, the twenty-sixth and last. At first they had quiet, for those were the days of the Watchful Peace, during which Sauron withdrew before the power of the White Council and the Ringwraiths remained hidden in Morgul Vale. But from the time of Denethor I, there was never full peace again, and even when Gondor had no great or open war its borders were under constant threat.

In the last years of Denethor I the race of uruks, black orcs of great strength, first appeared out of Mordor, and in 2475 they swept across Ithilien and took Osgiliath. Boromir son of Denethor (after whom Boromir of the Nine Walkers was later named) defeated them and regained Ithilien; but Osgiliath was finally ruined, and its great stone-bridge was broken. No people dwelt there afterwards. Boromir was a great captain, and even the Witch-king feared him. He was noble and fair of face, a man strong in body and in will, but he received a Morgul-wound in that war which shortened his days, and he became shrunken with pain and died twelve years after his father.

After him began the long rule of Cirion. He was watchful and wary, but the reach of Gondor had grown short, and he could do little more than defend his borders, while his enemies (or the power that moved them) prepared strokes against him that he could not hinder. The Corsairs harried his coasts, but it was in the north that his chief peril lay. In the wide lands of Rhovanion, between Mirkwood and the River Running, a fierce people now dwelt, wholly under the shadow of Dol Guldur. Often they made raids through the forest, until the vale of Anduin south of the Gladden was largely deserted. These Balchoth were constantly increased by others of like kind that came in from the east, whereas the people of Calenardhon had dwindled. Cirion was hard put to it to hold the line of the Anduin.

'Foreseeing the storm, Cirion sent north for aid, but over-late; for in that year (2510) the Balchoth, having built many great boats and rafts on the east shores of Anduin, swarmed over the River and swept away the defenders. An army marching up from the south was cut off and driven north over the Limlight, and there it was suddenly attacked by a horde of Orcs from the Mountains and pressed towards the Anduin. Then out of the North there came help beyond hope, and the horns of the Rohirrim were first heard in Gondor. Eorl the Young came with his riders and swept away the enemy, and pursued the Balchoth to the death over the fields of Calenardhon. Cirion granted to Eorl that land to dwell in, and he swore to Cirion the Oath of Eorl, of friendship at need or at call to the Lords of Gondor.'

In the days of Beren, the nineteenth Steward, an even greater peril came upon Gondor. Three great fleets, long prepared, came up from Umbar and the Harad, and assailed the coasts of Gondor in great force; and the enemy made many landings, even as far north as the mouth of the Isen. At the same time the Rohirrim were assailed from the west and the east, and their land was overrun, and they were driven into the dales of the White Mountains. In that year (2758) the Long Winter began with cold and great snows out of the North and the East which lasted for almost five months. Helm of Rohan and both his sons perished in that war; and there was misery and death in Eriador and in Rohan. But in Gondor south of the mountains things were less evil, and before spring came Beregond son of Beren had overcome the invaders. At once he sent aid to Rohan. He was the greatest captain that had arisen in Gondor since Boromir; and when he succeeded his father (2763) Gondor began to recover its strength. But Rohan was slower to be healed of the hurts that it had received. It was for this reason that Beren welcomed Saruman, and gave to him the keys of Orthanc; and from that year on (2759) Saruman dwelt in Isengard.

It was in the days of Beregond that the War of the Dwarves and Orcs was fought in the Misty Mountains (2793–9), of which only rumour came south, until the Orcs fleeing from Nanduhirion attempted to cross Rohan and establish themselves in the White Mountains. There was fighting for many years in the dales before that danger was ended.

When Belecthor II, the twenty-first Steward, died, the White Tree died also in Minas Tirith; but it was left standing 'until the King returns', for no seedling could be found.

In the days of Túrin II the enemies of Gondor began to move again; for Sauron was grown again to power and the day of his arising was drawing near. All but the hardiest of its people deserted Ithilien and removed west over Anduin, for the land was infested by Mordor-orcs. It was Túrin that built secret refuges for his soldiers in Ithilien, of which Henneth Annûn was the longest guarded and manned. He also fortified again the isle of Cair Andros[1] to defend Anórien. But his chief peril lay in the south, where the Haradrim had occupied South Gondor, and there was much fighting along the Poros. When Ithilien was invaded in great strength, King Folcwine of Rohan fulfilled the Oath of Eorl and repaid his debt for the aid brought by Beregond, sending many men to Gondor. With their aid Túrin won a victory at the crossing of the Poros; but the sons of Folcwine both fell in the battle. The Riders buried them after the fashion of their people, and they were laid in one mound, for they were twin brothers. Long it stood, *Haudh in Gwanur*, high upon the shore of the river, and the enemies of Gondor feared to pass it.

Turgon followed Túrin, but of his time it is chiefly remembered that two years ere his death, Sauron arose again, and declared himself openly; and he re-entered Mordor long prepared for him. Then the Barad-dûr was raised once more, and Mount Doom burst into flame, and the last of the folk of Ithilien fled far away. When Turgon died Saruman took Isengard for his own, and fortified it.

'Ecthelion II, son of Turgon, was a man of wisdom. With what power was left to him he began to strengthen his realm against the assault of Mordor. He encouraged all men of worth from near or far to enter his service, and to those who proved trustworthy he gave rank and reward. In much that he did he had the aid and advice of a great captain whom he loved above all. Thorongil men called him in Gondor, the Eagle of the Star, for he was swift and keen-eyed, and wore a silver star upon his cloak; but no one knew his true name nor in what land he was born. He came to Ecthelion from Rohan, where he had served the King Thengel, but he was not one of the Rohirrim. He was a great leader of men, by land or by sea, but he departed into the shadows whence he came, before the days of Ecthelion were ended.

---

[1] This name means 'Ship of Long-foam'; for the isle was shaped like a great ship, with a high prow pointing north, against which the white foam of Anduin broke on sharp rocks.

'Thorongil often counselled Ecthelion that the strength of the rebels in Umbar was a great peril to Gondor, and a threat to the fiefs of the south that would prove deadly, if Sauron moved to open war. At last he got leave of the Steward and gathered a small fleet, and he came to Umbar unlooked for by night, and there burned a great part of the ships of the Corsairs. He himself overthrew the Captain of the Haven in battle upon the quays, and then he withdrew his fleet with small loss. But when they came back to Pelargir, to men's grief and wonder, he would not return to Minas Tirith, where great honour awaited him.

'He sent a message of farewell to Ecthelion, saying: "Other tasks now call me, lord, and much time and many perils must pass, ere I come again to Gondor, if that be my fate." Though none could guess what those tasks might be, nor what summons he had received, it was known whither he went. For he took boat and crossed over Anduin, and there he said farewell to his companions and went on alone; and when he was last seen his face was towards the Mountains of Shadow.

'There was dismay in the City at the departure of Thorongil, and to all men it seemed a great loss, unless it were to Denethor, the son of Ecthelion, a man now ripe for the Stewardship, to which after four years he succeeded on the death of his father.

'Denethor II was a proud man, tall, valiant, and more kingly than any man that had appeared in Gondor for many lives of men; and he was wise also, and far-sighted, and learned in lore. Indeed he was as like to Thorongil as to one of nearest kin, and yet was ever placed second to the stranger in the hearts of men and the esteem of his father. At the time many thought that Thorongil had departed before his rival became his master; though indeed Thorongil had never himself vied with Denethor, nor held himself higher than the servant of his father. And in one matter only were their counsels to the Steward at variance: Thorongil often warned Ecthelion not to put trust in Saruman the White in Isengard, but to welcome rather Gandalf the Grey. But there was little love between Denethor and Gandalf; and after the days of Ecthelion there was less welcome for the Grey Pilgrim in Minas Tirith. Therefore later, when all was made clear, many believed that Denethor, who was subtle in mind and looked further and deeper than other men of his day, had discovered who this stranger Thorongil in truth was, and suspected that he and Mithrandir designed to supplant him.

'When Denethor became Steward (2984) he proved a masterful lord, holding the rule of all things in his own hand. He said little. He listened to counsel, and then followed his own mind. He had married late (2976), taking as wife Finduilas, daughter of Adrahil of Dol Amroth. She was a lady of great beauty and gentle heart, but before twelve years had passed she died. Denethor loved her, in his fashion, more dearly than any other, unless it were the elder of the sons that she bore him. But it seemed to men that she withered in the guarded city, as a flower of the seaward vales set upon a barren rock. The shadow in the east filled her with horror, and she turned her eyes ever south to the sea that she missed.

'After her death Denethor became more grim and silent than before, and would sit long alone in his tower deep in thought, foreseeing that the assault of Mordor would come in his time. It was afterwards believed that needing knowledge, but being proud, and trusting in his own strength of will, he dared to look in the *palantír* of the White Tower. None of the Stewards had dared to do this, nor even the kings Eärnil and Eärnur, after the fall of Minas Ithil when the *palantír* of Isildur came into the hands of the Enemy; for the Stone of Minas Tirith was the *palantír* of Anárion, most close in accord with the one that Sauron possessed.

'In this way Denethor gained his great knowledge of things that passed in his realm, and far beyond his borders, at which men marvelled; but he bought the knowledge dearly, being aged before his time by his contest with the will of Sauron. Thus pride increased in Denethor together with despair, until he saw in all the deeds of that time only a single combat between the Lord of the White Tower and the Lord of the Barad-dûr, and mistrusted all others who resisted Sauron, unless they served himself alone.

'So time drew on to the War of the Ring, and the sons of Denethor grew to manhood. Boromir, five years the elder, beloved by his father, was like him in face and pride, but in little else. Rather he was a man after the sort of King Eärnur of old, taking no wife and delighting chiefly in arms; fearless and strong, but caring little for lore, save the tales of old battles. Faramir the younger was like him in looks but otherwise in mind. He read the hearts of men as shrewdly as his father, but what he read moved him sooner to pity than to scorn. He was gentle in bearing, and a lover of lore and of music, and therefore by many in those days his courage was judged less than his brother's. But it was not so, except that he did not seek glory in danger without a purpose. He welcomed Gandalf at such times as he came to the City, and he learned what he could from his wisdom; and in this as in many other matters he displeased his father.

'Yet between the brothers there was great love, and had been since childhood, when Boromir was the helper and protector of Faramir. No jealousy or rivalry had arisen between them since, for their father's favour or for the praise of men. It did not seem possible to Faramir that any one in Gondor could rival Boromir, heir of Denethor, Captain of the White Tower; and of like mind was Boromir. Yet it proved otherwise at the test. But of all that befell these three in the War of the Ring much is said elsewhere. And after the War the days of the Ruling Stewards came to an end; for the heir of Isildur and Anárion returned and the kingship was renewed, and the standard of the White Tree flew once more from the Tower of Ecthelion.'

(v)
HERE FOLLOWS A PART OF THE TALE OF ARAGORN AND ARWEN

'Arador was the grandfather of the King. His son Arathorn sought in marriage Gilraen the Fair, daughter of Dírhael, who was himself a descendant of Aranarth. To this marriage Dírhael was opposed; for Gilraen was young and had not reached the age at which the women of the Dúnedain were accustomed to marry.

'"Moreover," he said, "Arathorn is a stern man of full age, and will be chieftain sooner than men looked for; yet my heart forebodes that he will be short-lived."

'But Ivorwen, his wife, who was also foresighted, answered:

"The more need of haste! The days are darkening before the storm, and great things are to come. If these two wed now, hope may be born for our people; but if they delay, it will not come while this age lasts."

'And it happened that when Arathorn and Gilraen had been married only one year, Arador was taken by hill-trolls in the Coldfells north of Rivendell and was slain; and Arathorn became Chieftain of the Dúnedain. The next year Gilraen bore him a son, and he was called Aragorn. But Aragorn was only two years old when Arathorn went riding against the Orcs with the sons of Elrond, and he was slain by an orc-arrow that pierced his eye; and so he proved indeed short-lived for one of his race, being but sixty years old when he fell.

'Then Aragorn, being now the Heir of Isildur, was taken with his mother to dwell in the house of Elrond; and Elrond took the place of his father and came to love him as a son of his own. But he was called Estel, that is "Hope", and his true name and lineage were kept secret at the bidding of Elrond; for the Wise then knew that the Enemy was seeking to discover the Heir of Isildur, if any remained upon earth.

'But when Estel was only twenty years of age, it chanced that he returned to Rivendell after great deeds in the company of the sons of Elrond; and Elrond looked at him and was pleased, for he saw that he was fair and noble and was early come to manhood, though he would yet become greater in body and in mind. That day therefore Elrond called him by his true name, and told him who he was and whose son; and he delivered to him the heirlooms of his house.

'"Here is the ring of Barahir," he said, "the token of our kinship from afar; and here also are the shards of Narsil. With these you may yet do great deeds; for I foretell that the span of your life shall be greater than the measure of Men, unless evil befalls you or you fail at the test. But the test will be hard and long. The Sceptre of Annúminas I withhold, for you have yet to earn it."

'The next day at the hour of sunset Aragorn walked alone in the woods, and his heart was high within him; and he sang, for he was full of hope and the world was fair. And suddenly even as he sang he saw a maiden walking on a greensward among the white stems of the birches; and he halted amazed, thinking that he had strayed into a dream, or else that he had received the gift of the Elf-minstrels, who can make the things of which they sing appear before the eyes of those that listen.

'For Aragorn had been singing a part of the Lay of Lúthien which tells of the meeting of Lúthien and Beren in the forest of Neldoreth. And behold! there Lúthien walked before his eyes in Rivendell, clad in a mantle of silver and blue, fair as the twilight in Elven-home; her dark hair strayed in a sudden wind, and her brows were bound with gems like stars.

'For a moment Aragorn gazed in silence, but fearing that she would pass away and never be seen again, he called to her crying, *Tinúviel, Tinúviel!* even as Beren had done in the Elder Days long ago.

'Then the maiden turned to him and smiled, and she said: "Who are you? And why do you call me by that name?"

'And he answered: "Because I believed you to be indeed Lúthien Tinúviel, of whom I was singing. But if you are not she, then you walk in her likeness."

' "So many have said," she answered gravely. "Yet her name is not mine. Though maybe my doom will be not unlike hers. But who are you?"

' "Estel I was called," he said; "but I am Aragorn, Arathorn's son, Isildur's Heir, Lord of the Dúnedain"; yet even in the saying he felt that this high lineage, in which his heart had rejoiced, was now of little worth, and as nothing compared to her dignity and loveliness.

'But she laughed merrily and said: "Then we are akin from afar. For I am Arwen Elrond's daughter, and am named also Undómiel."

' "Often is it seen," said Aragorn, "that in dangerous days men hide their chief treasure. Yet I marvel at Elrond and your brothers; for though I have dwelt in this house from childhood, I have heard no word of you. How comes it that we have never met before? Surely your father has not kept you locked in his hoard?"

' "No," she said, and looked up at the Mountains that rose in the east. "I have dwelt for a time in the land of my mother's kin, in far Lothlórien. I have but lately returned to visit my father again. It is many years since I walked in Imladris."

'Then Aragorn wondered, for she had seemed of no greater age than he, who had lived yet no more than a score of years in Middle-earth. But Arwen looked in his eyes and said: "Do not wonder! For the children of Elrond have the life of the Eldar."

'Then Aragorn was abashed, for he saw the elven-light in her eyes and the wisdom of many days; yet from that hour he loved Arwen Undómiel daughter of Elrond.

'In the days that followed Aragorn fell silent, and his mother perceived that some strange thing had befallen him; and at last he yielded to her questions and told her of the meeting in the twilight of the trees.

' "My son," said Gilraen, "your aim is high, even for the descendant of many kings. For this lady is the noblest and fairest that now walks the earth. And it is not fit that mortal should wed with the Elf-kin."

' "Yet we have some part in that kinship," said Aragorn, "if the tale of my forefathers is true that I have learned."

' "It is true," said Gilraen, "but that was long ago and in another age of this world, before our race was diminished. Therefore I am afraid; for without the good will of Master Elrond the Heirs of Isildur will soon come to an end. But I do not think that you will have the good will of Elrond in this matter."

' "Then bitter will my days be, and I will walk in the wild alone," said Aragorn.

' "That will indeed be your fate," said Gilraen; but though she had in a measure the foresight of her people, she said no more to him of her foreboding, nor did she speak to any one of what her son had told her.

'But Elrond saw many things and read many hearts. One day, therefore, before the fall of the year he called Aragorn to his chamber, and he said: "Aragorn, Arathorn's son, Lord of the Dúnedain, listen to me! A great doom awaits you, either to rise above the height of all your fathers since the days of Elendil, or to fall into darkness with all that is left of your kin. Many years of trial lie before you. You shall neither have wife, nor bind any woman to you in troth, until your time comes and you are found worthy of it."

'Then Aragorn was troubled, and he said: "Can it be that my mother has spoken of this?"

'"No indeed," said Elrond. "Your own eyes have betrayed you. But I do not speak of my daughter alone. You shall be betrothed to no man's child as yet. But as for Arwen the Fair, Lady of Imladris and of Lórien, Evenstar of her people, she is of lineage greater than yours, and she has lived in the world already so long that to her you are but as a yearling shoot beside a young birch of many summers. She is too far above you. And so, I think, it may well seem to her. But even if it were not so, and her heart turned towards you, I should still be grieved because of the doom that is laid on us."

'"What is that doom?" said Aragorn.

'"That so long as I abide here, she shall live with the youth of the Eldar," answered Elrond, "and when I depart, she shall go with me, if she so chooses."

'"I see," said Aragorn, "that I have turned my eyes to a treasure no less dear than the treasure of Thingol that Beren once desired. Such is my fate." Then suddenly the foresight of his kindred came to him, and he said: "But lo! Master Elrond, the years of your abiding run short at last, and the choice must soon be laid on your children, to part either with you or with Middle-earth."

'"Truly," said Elrond. "Soon, as we account it, though many years of Men must still pass. But there will be no choice before Arwen, my beloved, unless you, Aragorn, Arathorn's son, come between us and bring one of us, you or me, to a bitter parting beyond the end of the world. You do not know yet what you desire of me." He sighed, and after a while, looking gravely upon the young man, he said again: "The years will bring what they will. We will speak no more of this until many have passed. The days darken, and much evil is to come."

'Then Aragorn took leave lovingly of Elrond; and the next day he said farewell to his mother, and to the house of Elrond, and to Arwen, and he went out into the wild. For nearly thirty years he laboured in the cause against Sauron; and he became a friend of Gandalf the Wise, from whom he gained much wisdom. With him he made many perilous journeys, but as the years wore on

he went more often alone. His ways were hard and long, and
he became somewhat grim to look upon, unless he chanced to
smile; and yet he seemed to Men worthy of honour, as a king
that is in exile, when he did not hide his true shape. For he went
in many guises, and won renown under many names. He rode
in the host of the Rohirrim, and fought for the Lord of Gondor
by land and by sea; and then in the hour of victory he passed
out of the knowledge of Men of the West, and went alone far
into the East and deep into the South, exploring the hearts of
Men, both evil and good, and uncovering the plots and devices
of the servants of Sauron.

'Thus he became at last the most hardy of living Men, skilled
in their crafts and lore, and was yet more than they; for he was
elven-wise, and there was a light in his eyes that when they were
kindled few could endure. His face was sad and stern because
of the doom that was laid on him, and yet hope dwelt ever in
the depths of his heart, from which mirth would arise at times
like a spring from the rock.

'It came to pass that when Aragorn was nine and forty years of
age he returned from perils on the dark confines of Mordor,
where Sauron now dwelt again and was busy with evil. He was
weary and he wished to go back to Rivendell and rest there for
a while ere he journeyed into the far countries; and on his way
he came to the borders of Lórien and was admitted to the hidden
land by the Lady Galadriel.

'He did not know it, but Arwen Undómiel was also there,
dwelling again for a time with the kin of her mother. She was
little changed, for the mortal years had passed her by; yet her
face was more grave, and her laughter now seldom was heard.
But Aragorn was grown to full stature of body and mind, and
Galadriel bade him cast aside his wayworn raiment, and she
clothed him in silver and white, with a cloak of elven-grey and
a bright gem on his brow. Then more than any kind of Men he
appeared, and seemed rather an Elf-lord from the Isles of the
West. And thus it was that Arwen first beheld him again after
their long parting; and as he came walking towards her under
the trees of Caras Galadhon laden with flowers of gold, her
choice was made and her doom appointed.

'Then for a season they wandered together in the glades of Lothlórien, until it was time for him to depart. And on the evening of Midsummer Aragorn, Arathorn's son, and Arwen daughter of Elrond went to the fair hill, Cerin Amroth, in the midst of the land, and they walked unshod on the undying grass with elanor and niphredil about their feet. And there upon that hill they looked east to the Shadow and west to the Twilight, and they plighted their troth and were glad.

'And Arwen said: "Dark is the Shadow, and yet my heart rejoices; for you, Estel, shall be among the great whose valour will destroy it."

'But Aragorn answered: "Alas! I cannot foresee it, and how it may come to pass is hidden from me. Yet with your hope I will hope. And the Shadow I utterly reject. But neither, lady, is the Twilight for me; for I a mortal, and if you will cleave to me, Evenstar, then the Twilight you must also renounce."

'And she stood then as still as a white tree, looking into the West, and at last she said: "I will cleave to you, Dúnadan, and turn from the Twilight. Yet there lies the land of my people and the long home of all my kin." She loved her father dearly.

'When Elrond learned the choice of his daughter, he was silent, though his heart was grieved and found the doom long feared none the easier to endure. But when Aragorn came again to Rivendell he called him to him, and he said:

'"My son, years come when hope will fade, and beyond them little is clear to me. And now a shadow lies between us. Maybe, it has been appointed so, that by my loss the kingship of Men may be restored. Therefore, though I love you, I say to you: Arwen Undómiel shall not diminish her life's grace for less cause. She shall not be the bride of any Man less than the King of both Gondor and Arnor. To me then even our victory can bring only sorrow and parting – but to you hope of joy for a while. Alas, my son! I fear that to Arwen the Doom of Men may seem hard at the ending."

'So it stood afterwards between Elrond and Aragorn, and they spoke no more of this matter; but Aragorn went forth again to danger and toil. And while the world darkened and fear fell on Middle-earth, as the power of Sauron grew and the Barad-dûr rose ever taller and stronger, Arwen remained in Rivendell, and when Aragorn was abroad, from afar she watched over him in thought; and in hope she made for him a great and kingly standard, such as only one might display who claimed the lordship of the Númenoreans and the inheritance of Elendil.

'After a few years Gilraen took leave of Elrond and returned to her own people in Eriador, and lived alone; and she seldom saw her son again, for he spent many years in far countries. But on a time, when Aragorn had returned to the North, he came to her, and she said to him before he went:

' "This is our last parting, Estel, my son. I am aged by care, even as one of lesser Men; and now that it draws near I cannot face the darkness of our time that gathers upon Middle-earth. I shall leave it soon."

'Aragorn tried to comfort her, saying: "Yet there may be a light beyond the darkness; and if so, I would have you see it and be glad."

'But she answered only with this *linnod*:

> *Onen i-Estel Edain, ú-chebin estel anim,*[1]

and Aragorn went away heavy of heart. Gilraen died before the next spring.

'Thus the years drew on to the War of the Ring; of which more is told elsewhere: how the means unforeseen was revealed whereby Sauron might be overthrown, and how hope beyond hope was fulfilled. And it came to pass that in the hour of defeat Aragorn came up from the sea and unfurled the standard of Arwen in the battle of the Fields of Pelennor, and in that day he was first hailed as king. And at last when all was done he entered into the inheritance of his fathers and received the crown of Gondor and sceptre of Arnor; and at Midsummer in the year of the Fall of Sauron he took the hand of Arwen Undómiel, and they were wedded in the city of the Kings.

'The Third Age ended thus in victory and hope; and yet grievous among the sorrows of that Age was the parting of Elrond and Arwen, for they were sundered by the Sea and by a doom beyond the end of the world. When the Great Ring was

[1] 'I gave Hope to the Dúnedain, I have kept no hope for myself.'

unmade and the Three were shorn of their power, then Elrond
grew weary at last and forsook Middle-earth, never to return.
But Arwen became as a mortal woman, and yet it was not her
lot to die until all that she had gained was lost.

'As Queen of Elves and Men she dwelt with Aragorn for
six-score years in great glory and bliss; yet at last he felt the
approach of old age and knew that the span of his life-days was
drawing to an end, long though it had been. Then Aragorn said
to Arwen:

'"At last, Lady Evenstar, fairest in this world, and most
beloved, my world is fading. Lo! we have gathered, and we have
spent, and now the time of payment draws near."

'Arwen knew well what he intended, and long had foreseen
it; nonetheless she was overborne by her grief. "Would you then,
lord, before your time leave your people that live by your word?"
she said.

'"Not before my time," he answered. "For if I will not go
now, then I must soon go perforce. And Eldarion our son is a
man full-ripe for kingship."

'Then going to the House of the Kings in the Silent Street,
Aragorn laid him down on the long bed that had been prepared
for him. There he said farewell to Eldarion, and gave into his
hands the winged crown of Gondor and the sceptre of Arnor;
and then all left him save Arwen, and she stood alone by his
bed. And for all her wisdom and lineage she could not forbear
to plead with him to stay yet for a while. She was not yet weary
of her days, and thus she tasted the bitterness of the mortality
that she had taken upon her.

'"Lady Undómiel," said Aragorn, "the hour is indeed hard,
yet it was made even in that day when we met under the white
birches in the garden of Elrond where none now walk. And on
the hill of Cerin Amroth when we forsook both the Shadow and
the Twilight this doom we accepted. Take counsel with yourself,
beloved, and ask whether you would indeed have me wait until
I wither and fall from my high seat unmanned and witless. Nay,
lady, I am the last of the Númenoreans and the latest King of
the Elder Days; and to me has been given not only a span thrice
that of Men of Middle-earth, but also the grace to go at my will,
and give back the gift. Now, therefore, I will sleep.

' "I speak no comfort to you, for there is no comfort for such pain within the circles of the world. The uttermost choice is before you: to repent and go to the Havens and bear away into the West the memory of our days together that shall there be evergreen but never more than memory; or else to abide the Doom of Men."

' "Nay, dear lord," she said, "that choice is long over. There is now no ship that would bear me hence, and I must indeed abide the Doom of Men, whether I will or I nill: the loss and the silence. But I say to you, King of the Númenoreans, not till now have I understood the tale of your people and their fall. As wicked fools I scorned them, but I pity them at last. For if this is indeed, as the Eldar say, the gift of the One to Men, it is bitter to receive."

' "So it seems," he said. "But let us not be overthrown at the final test, who of old renounced the Shadow and the Ring. In sorrow we must go, but not in despair. Behold! we are not bound for ever to the circles of the world, and beyond them is more than memory. Farewell!"

' "Estel, Estel!" she cried, and with that even as he took her hand and kissed it, he fell into sleep. Then a great beauty was revealed in him, so that all who after came there looked on him in wonder; for they saw that the grace of his youth, and the valour of his manhood, and the wisdom and majesty of his age were blended together. And long there he lay, an image of the splendour of the Kings of Men in glory undimmed before the breaking of the world.

'But Arwen went forth from the House, and the light of her eyes was quenched, and it seemed to her people that she had become cold and grey as nightfall in winter that comes without a star. Then she said farewell to Eldarion, and to her daughters, and to all whom she had loved; and she went out from the city of Minas Tirith and passed away to the land of Lórien, and dwelt there alone under the fading trees until winter came. Galadriel had passed away and Celeborn also was gone, and the land was silent.

'There at last when the mallorn-leaves were falling, but spring had not yet come,[1] she laid herself to rest upon Cerin Amroth;

---

[1] II, p. 156.

and there is her green grave, until the world is changed, and all the days of her life are utterly forgotten by men that come after, and elanor and niphredil bloom no more east of the Sea.

'Here ends this tale, as it has come to us from the South; and with the passing of Evenstar no more is said in this book of the days of old.'

II
THE HOUSE OF EORL

'Eorl the Young was lord of the Men of Éothéod. That land lay near the sources of Anduin, between the furthest ranges of the Misty Mountains and the northernmost parts of Mirkwood. The Éothéod had moved to those regions in the days of King Eärnil II from lands in the vales of Anduin between the Carrock and the Gladden, and they were in origin close akin to the Beornings and the men of the west-eaves of the forest. The forefathers of Eorl claimed descent from kings of Rhovanion, whose realm lay beyond Mirkwood before the invasions of the Wainriders, and thus they accounted themselves kinsmen of the kings of Gondor descended from Eldacar. They loved best the plains, and delighted in horses and in all feats of horsemanship, but there were many men in the middle vales of Anduin in those days, and moreover the shadow of Dol Guldur was lengthening; when therefore they heard of the overthrow of the Witch-king, they sought more room in the North, and drove away the remnants of the people of Angmar on the east side of the Mountains. But in the days of Léod, father of Eorl, they had grown to be a numerous people and were again somewhat straitened in the land of their home.

'In the two thousand five hundred and tenth year of the Third Age a new peril threatened Gondor. A great host of wild men from the North-east swept over Rhovanion and coming down out of the Brown-lands crossed the Anduin on rafts. At the same time by chance or design the Orcs (who at that time before their war with the Dwarves were in great strength) made a descent from the Mountains. The invaders overran Calenardhon, and

Cirion, Steward of Gondor, sent north for help; for there had
been long friendship between the Men of Anduin's Vale and the
people of Gondor. But in the valley of the River men were now
few and scattered, and slow to render such aid as they could.
At last tidings came to Eorl of the need of Gondor, and late
though it seemed, he set out with a great host of riders.

'Thus he came to the battle of the Field of Celebrant, for that
was the name of the green land that lay between Silverlode
and Limlight. There the northern army of Gondor was in peril.
Defeated in the Wold and cut off from the south, it had been
driven across the Limlight, and was then suddenly assailed by
the Orc-host that pressed it towards the Anduin. All hope was
lost when, unlooked for, the Riders came out of the North and
broke upon the rear of the enemy. Then the fortunes of battle
were reversed, and the enemy was driven with slaughter over
Limlight. Eorl led his men in pursuit, and so great was the fear
that went before the horsemen of the North that the invaders of
the Wold were also thrown into panic, and the Riders hunted
them over the plains of Calenardhon.'

The people of that region had become few since the Plague,
and most of those that remained had been slaughtered by the
savage Easterlings. Cirion, therefore, in reward for his aid, gave
Calenardhon between Anduin and Isen to Eorl and his people;
and they sent north for their wives and children and their goods
and settled in that land. They named it anew the Mark of the
Riders, and they called themselves the Eorlingas; but in Gondor
their land was called Rohan, and its people the Rohirrim (that
is, the Horse-lords). Thus Eorl became the first King of the
Mark, and he chose for his dwelling a green hill before the feet
of the White Mountains that were the south-wall of his land.
There the Rohirrim lived afterwards as free men under their
own kings and laws, but in perpetual alliance with Gondor.

'Many lords and warriors, and many fair and valiant women,
are named in the songs of Rohan that still remember the North.
Frumgar, they say, was the name of the chieftain who led his
people to Éothéod. Of his son, Fram, they tell that he slew
Scatha, the great dragon of Ered Mithrin, and the land had peace
from the long-worms afterwards. Thus Fram won great wealth,

but was at feud with the Dwarves, who claimed the hoard of Scatha. Fram would not yield them a penny, and sent to them instead the teeth of Scatha made into a necklace, saying: "Jewels such as these you will not match in your treasuries, for they are hard to come by." Some say that the Dwarves slew Fram for this insult. There was no great love between Éothéod and the Dwarves.

'Léod was the name of Eorl's father. He was a tamer of wild horses; for there were many at that time in the land. He captured a white foal and it grew quickly to a horse strong, and fair, and proud. No man could tame it. When Léod dared to mount it, it bore him away, and at last threw him, and Léod's head struck a rock, and so he died. He was then only two and forty years old, and his son a youth of sixteen.

'Eorl vowed that he would avenge his father. He hunted long for the horse, and at last he caught sight of him; and his companions expected that he would try to come within bowshot and kill him. But when they drew near, Eorl stood up and called in a loud voice: "Come hither, Mansbane, and get a new name!" To their wonder the horse looked towards Eorl, and came and stood before him, and Eorl said: "Felaróf I name you. You loved your freedom, and I do not blame you for that. But now you owe me a great weregild, and you shall surrender your freedom to me until your life's end."

'Then Eorl mounted him, and Felaróf submitted; and Eorl rode him home without bit or bridle; and he rode him in like fashion ever after. The horse understood all that men said, though he would allow no man but Eorl to mount him. It was upon Felaróf that Eorl rode to the Field of Celebrant; for that horse proved as long lived as Men, and so were his descendants. These were the *mearas*, who would bear no one but the King of the Mark or his sons, until the time of Shadowfax. Men said of them that Béma (whom the Eldar call Oromë) must have brought their sire from West over Sea.

'Of the Kings of the Mark between Eorl and Théoden most is said of Helm Hammerhand. He was a grim man of great strength. There was at that time a man named Freca, who claimed descent from King Fréawine, though he had, men said, much Dunlendish blood, and was dark-haired. He grew rich and powerful, having wide lands on either side of the Adorn.[1] Near its source he made himself a stronghold and paid little heed to the king. Helm mistrusted him, but called him to his councils; and he came when it pleased him.

'To one of these councils Freca rode with many men, and he asked the hand of Helm's daughter for his son Wulf. But Helm said: "You have grown big since you were last here; but it is mostly fat, I guess"; and men laughed at that, for Freca was wide in the belt.

'Then Freca fell in a rage and reviled the king, and said this at the last: "Old kings that refuse a proffered staff may fall on their knees." Helm answered: "Come! The marriage of your son is a trifle. Let Helm and Freca deal with it later. Meanwhile the king and his council have matters of moment to consider."

'When the council was over, Helm stood up and laid his great hand on Freca's shoulder, saying: "The king does not permit brawls in his house, but men are freer outside"; and he forced Freca to walk before him out from Edoras into the field. To Freca's men that came up he said: "Be off! We need no hearers. We are going to speak of a private matter alone. Go and talk to my men!" And they looked and saw that the king's men and his friends far outnumbered them, and they drew back.

'"Now, Dunlending," said the king, "you have only Helm to deal with, alone and unarmed. But you have said much already, and it is my turn to speak. Freca, your folly has grown with your belly. You talk of a staff! If Helm dislikes a crooked staff that is thrust on him, he breaks it. So!" With that he smote Freca such a blow with his fist that he fell back stunned, and died soon after.

'Helm then proclaimed Freca's son and near kin the king's enemies; and they fled, for at once Helm sent many men riding to the west marches.'

Four years later (2758) great troubles came to Rohan, and no help could be sent from Gondor, for three fleets of the Corsairs attacked it and there was war on all its coasts. At the same time

---

[1] It flows into Isen from the west of Ered Nimrais.

Rohan was again invaded from the East, and the Dunlendings seeing their chance came over the Isen and down from Isengard. It was soon known that Wulf was their leader. The were in great force, for they were joined by enemies of Gondor that landed in the mouths of Lefnui and Isen.

The Rohirrim were defeated and their land was overrun; and those who were not slain or enslaved fled to the dales of the mountains. Helm was driven back with great loss from the Crossings of Isen and took refuge in the Hornburg and the ravine behind (which was after known as Helm's Deep). There he was besieged. Wulf took Edoras and sat in Meduseld and called himself king. There Haleth Helm's son fell, last of all, defending the doors.

'Soon afterwards the Long Winter began, and Rohan lay under snow for nearly five months (November to March, 2758–9). Both the Rohirrim and their foes suffered grievously in the cold, and in the dearth that lasted longer. In Helm's Deep there was a great hunger after Yule; and being in despair, against the king's counsel, Háma his younger son led men out on a sortie and foray, but they were lost in the snow. Helm grew fierce and gaunt for famine and grief; and the dread of him alone was worth many men in the defence of the Burg. He would go out by himself, clad in white, and stalk like a snow-troll into the camps of his enemies, and slay many men with his hands. It was believed that if he bore no weapon no weapon would bite on him. The Dunlendings said that if he could find no food he ate men. That tale lasted long in Dunland. Helm had a great horn, and soon it was marked that before he sallied forth he would blow a blast upon it that echoed in the Deep; and then so great a fear fell on his enemies that instead of gathering to take him or kill him they fled away down the Coomb.

'One night men heard the horn blowing, but Helm did not return. In the morning there came a sun-gleam, the first for long days, and they saw a white figure standing still on the Dike, alone, for none of the Dunlendings dared come near. There stood Helm, dead as a stone, but his knees were unbent. Yet men said that the horn was still heard at times in the Deep and the wraith of Helm would walk among the foes of Rohan and kill men with fear.

'Soon after the winter broke. Then Fréaláf, son of Hild, Helm's sister, came down out of Dunharrow, to which many had fled; and with a small company of desperate men he surprised Wulf in Meduseld and slew him, and regained Edoras. There were great floods after the snows, and the vale of Entwash became a vast fen. The Eastern invaders perished or withdrew; and there came help at last from Gondor, by the roads both east and west of the mountains. Before the year (2759) was ended the Dunlendings were driven out, even from Isengard; and then Fréaláf became king.

'Helm was brought from the Hornburg and laid in the ninth mound. Ever after the white *simbelmynë* grew there most thickly, so that the mound seemed to be snow-clad. When Fréaláf died a new line of mounds was begun.'

The Rohirrim were grievously reduced by war and dearth and loss of cattle and horses; and it was well that no great danger threatened them again for many years, for it was not until the time of King Folcwine that they recovered their former strength.

It was at the crowning of Fréaláf that Saruman appeared, bringing gifts, and speaking great praise of the valour of the Rohirrim. All thought him a welcome guest. Soon after he took up his abode in Isengard. For this, Beren, Steward of Gondor, gave him leave, for Gondor still claimed Isengard as a fortress of its realm, and not part of Rohan. Beren also gave into Saruman's keeping the keys of Orthanc. That tower no enemy had been able to harm or to enter.

In this way Saruman began to behave as a lord of Men; for at first he held Isengard as a lieutenant of the Steward and warden of the tower. But Fréaláf was as glad as Beren to have this so, and to know that Isengard was in the hands of a strong friend. A friend he long seemed, and maybe in the beginning he was one in truth. Though afterwards there was little doubt in men's minds that Saruman went to Isengard in hope to find the Stone still there, and with the purpose of building up a power of his own. Certainly after the last White Council (2953) his designs towards Rohan, though he hid them, were evil. He then took Isengard for his own and began to make it a place of guarded strength and fear, as though to rival the Barad-dûr. His friends and servants he drew then from all who hated Gondor and Rohan, whether Men or other creatures more evil.

THE KINGS OF THE MARK

Year[1]   *First Line*

2485–2545   1. *Eorl the Young.* He was so named because he succeeded his father in youth and remained yellow-haired and ruddy to the end of his days. These were shortened by a renewed attack of the Easterlings. Eorl fell in battle in the Wold, and the first mound was raised. Felaróf was laid there also.

2512–70   2. *Brego.* He drove the enemy out of the Wold, and Rohan was not attacked again for many years. In 2569 he completed the great hall of Meduseld. At the feast his son Baldor vowed that he would tread 'the Paths of the Dead' and did not return.[2] Brego died of grief the next year.

2544–2645   3. *Aldor the Old.* He was Brego's second son. He became known as the Old, since he lived to a great age, and was king for 75 years. In his time the Rohirrim increased, and drove out or subdued the last of the Dunlendish people that lingered east of Isen. Harrowdale and other mountain-valleys were settled. Of the next three kings little is said, for Rohan had peace and prospered in their time.

2570–2659   4. *Fréa.* Eldest son, but fourth child of Aldor; he was already old when he became king.

2594–2680   5. *Fréawine.*

2619–99   6. *Goldwine.*

2644–2718   7. *Déor.* In his time the Dunlendings raided often over the Isen. In 2710 they occupied the deserted ring of Isengard, and could not be dislodged.

---

[1] The dates are given according to the reckoning of Gondor (Third Age). Those in the margin are of birth and death.

[2] V, pp. 59, 71.

2668–2741 8. *Gram.*

2691–2759 9. *Helm Hammerhand.* At the end of his reign Rohan suffered great loss, by invasion and the Long Winter. Helm and his sons Haleth and Háma perished. Fréaláf, Helm's sister's son, became king.

Year   *Second Line*

2726–2798 10. *Fréaláf Hildeson.* In his time Saruman came to Isengard, from which the Dunlendings had been driven. The Rohirrim at first profited by his friendship in the days of dearth and weakness that followed.

2752–2842 11. *Brytta.* He was called by his people *Léofa*, for he was loved by all; he was openhanded and a help to all the needy. In his time there was war with Orcs that, driven from the North, sought refuges in the White Mountains.[1] When he died it was thought that they had all been hunted out; but it was not so.

2780–2851 12. *Walda.* He was king only nine years. He was slain with all his companions when they were trapped by Orcs, as they rode by mountain-paths from Dunharrow.

2804–64   13. *Folca.* He was a great hunter, but he vowed to chase no wild beast while there was an Orc left in Rohan. When the last orc-hold was found and destroyed, he went to hunt the great boar of Everholt in the Firien Wood. He slew the boar but died of the tusk-wounds that it gave him.

2830–2903 14. *Folcwine.* When he became king the Rohirrim had recovered their strength. He reconquered the west-march (between Adorn and Isen) that Dunlendings had occupied. Rohan had received great help from Gondor in the evil days. When, therefore, he heard that the Haradrim were assailing

[1] VII, p. 35.

Gondor with great strength, he sent many men to
the help of the Steward. He wished to lead them
himself, but was dissuaded, and his twin sons
Folcred and Fastred (born 2858) went in his stead.
They fell side by side in battle in Ithilien (2885).
Túrin II of Gondor sent to Folcwine a rich weregild
of gold.

2870–2953 15. *Fengel*. He was the third son and fourth child
of Folcwine. He is not remembered with praise.
He was greedy of food and of gold, and at strife
with his marshals, and with his children. Thengel,
his third child and only son, left Rohan when he
came to manhood and lived long in Gondor, and
won honour in the service of Turgon.

2905–80 16. *Thengel*. He took no wife until late, but in 2943
he wedded Morwen of Lossarnach in Gondor,
though she was seventeen years the younger. She
bore him three children in Gondor, of whom
Théoden, the second, was his only son. When Fengel died the Rohirrim recalled him, and he returned
unwillingly. But he proved a good and wise king;
though the speech of Gondor was used in his
house, and not all men thought that good. Morwen
bore him two more daughters in Rohan; and the
last, Théodwyn, was the fairest, though she came
late (2963), the child of his age. Her brother loved
her dearly.

It was soon after Thengel's return that Saruman
declared himself Lord of Isengard and began to
give trouble to Rohan, encroaching on its borders
and supporting its enemies.

2948–3019 17. *Théoden*. He is called Théoden Ednew in the
lore of Rohan, for he fell into a decline under the
spells of Saruman, but was healed by Gandalf, and
in the last year of his life arose and led his men to
victory at the Hornburg, and soon after to the
Fields of Pelennor, the greatest battle of the Age.
He fell before the gates of Mundburg. For a while
he rested in the land of his birth, among the dead

Kings of Gondor, but was brought back and laid in the eighth mound of his line at Edoras. Then a new line was begun.

Third Line

In 2989 Théodwyn married Éomund of Eastfold, the chief Marshal of the Mark. Her son Éomer was born in 2991, and her daughter Éowyn in 2995. At that time Sauron had arisen again, and the shadow of Mordor reached out to Rohan. Orcs began to raid in the eastern regions and slay or steal horses. Others also came down from the Misty Mountains, many being great uruks in the service of Saruman, though it was long before that was suspected. Éomund's chief charge lay in the east marches; and he was a great lover of horses and hater of Orcs. If news came of a raid he would often ride against them in hot anger, unwarily and with few men. Thus it came about that he was slain in 3002; for he pursued a small band to the borders of the Emyn Muil, and was there surprised by a strong force that lay in wait in the rocks.

Not long after Théodwyn took sick and died to the great grief of the king. Her children he took into his house, calling them son and daughter. He had only one child of his own, Théodred his son, then twenty-four years old; for the queen Elfhild had died in childbirth, and Théoden did not wed again. Éomer and Éowyn grew up at Edoras and saw the dark shadow fall on the halls of Théoden. Éomer was like his fathers before him; but Éowyn was slender and tall, with a grace and pride that came to her out of the South from Morwen of Lossarnach, whom the Rohirrim had called Steelsheen.

2991–F.A. 63 (3084) *Éomer Éadig*. When still young he became a Marshal of the Mark (3017) and was given his father's charge in the east marches. In the War of the Ring Théodred fell in battle with Saruman at the Crossings of Isen. Therefore before he died on the Fields of the Pelennor Théoden named Éomer his heir and called him king. In that day Éowyn also won renown, for she fought in that battle, riding in disguise; and was known after in the Mark as the Lady of the Shield-arm.[1]

Éomer became a great king, and being young when he succeeded Théoden he reigned for sixty-five years, longer than all their kings before him save Aldor the Old. In the War of the Ring he made the friendship of King Elessar, and of Imrahil of Dol Amroth; and he rode often to Gondor. In the last year of the Third Age he wedded Lothíriel, daughter of Imrahil. Their son Elfwine the Fair ruled after him.

In Éomer's day in the Mark men had peace who wished for it, and the people increased both in the dales and the plains, and their horses multiplied. In Gondor the King Elessar now ruled, and in Arnor also. In all the lands of those realms of old he was king, save in Rohan only; for he renewed to Éomer the gift of Cirion, and Éomer took again the Oath of Eorl. Often he fulfilled it. For though Sauron had passed, the hatreds and evils that he bred had not died, and the King of the West had many enemies to subdue before the White Tree could grow in peace. And wherever King Elessar went with war King Éomer went with him; and beyond the Sea of Rhûn and on the far fields of the South the thunder of the cavalry of the Mark was heard, and the White Horse upon Green flew in many winds until Éomer grew old.

[1] For her shield-arm was broken by the mace of the Witch-king; but he was brought to nothing, and thus the words of Glorfindel long before to King Eärnur were fulfilled, that the Witch-king would not fall by the hand of man. For it is said in the songs of the Mark that in this deed Éowyn had the aid of Théoden's esquire, and that he also was not a Man but a Halfling out of a far country, though Éomer gave him honour in the Mark and the name of Holdwine.

[This Holdwine was none other than Meriadoc the Magnificent who was Master of Buckland.]

III
DURIN'S FOLK

Concerning the beginning of the Dwarves strange tales are told both by the Eldar and by the Dwarves themselves; but since these things lie far back beyond our days little is said of them here. Durin is the name that the Dwarves used for the eldest of the Seven Fathers of their race, and the ancestor of all the kings of the Longbeards.[1] He slept alone, until in the deeps of time and the awakening of that people he came to Azanulbizar, and in the caves above Kheled-zâram in the east of the Misty Mountains he made his dwelling, where afterwards were the Mines of Moria renowned in song.

There he lived so long that he was known far and wide as Durin the Deathless. Yet in the end he died before the Elder Days had passed, and his tomb was in Khazad-dûm; but his line never failed, and five times an heir was born in his House so like to his Forefather that he received the name of Durin. He was indeed held by the Dwarves to be the Deathless that returned; for they have many strange tales and beliefs concerning themselves and their fate in the world.

After the end of the First Age the power and wealth of Khazad-dûm was much increased; for it was enriched by many people and much lore and craft when the ancient cities of Nogrod and Belegost in the Blue Mountains were ruined at the breaking of Thangorodrim. The power of Moria endured throughout the Dark Years and the dominion of Sauron, for though Eregion was destroyed and the gates of Moria were shut, the halls of Khazad-dûm were too deep and strong and filled with a people too numerous and valiant for Sauron to conquer from without. Thus its wealth remained long unravished, though its people began to dwindle.

It came to pass that in the middle of the Third Age Durin was again its king, being the sixth of that name. The power of Sauron, servant of Morgoth, was then again growing in the world, though the Shadow in the Forest that looked towards

---

[1] *The Hobbit*, p. 50.

Moria was not yet known for what it was. All evil things were stirring. The Dwarves delved deep at that time, seeking beneath Barazinbar for *mithril*, the metal beyond price that was becoming yearly ever harder to win.[1] Thus they roused from sleep[2] a thing of terror that, flying from Thangorodrim, had lain hidden at the foundations of the earth since the coming of the Host of the West: a Balrog of Morgoth. Durin was slain by it, and the year after Náin I, his son; and then the glory of Moria passed, and its people were destroyed or fled far away.

Most of those that escaped made their way into the North, and Thráin I, Náin's son, came to Erebor, the Lonely Mountain, near the eastern eaves of Mirkwood, and there he began new works, and became King under the Mountain. In Erebor he found the great jewel, the Arkenstone, Heart of the Mountain.[3] But Thorin I his son removed and went into the far North to the Grey Mountains, where most of Durin's folk were now gathering; for those mountains were rich and little explored. But there were dragons in the wastes beyond; and after many years they became strong again and multiplied, and they made war on the Dwarves, and plundered their works. At last Dáin I, together with Frór his second son, was slain at the door of his hall by a great cold-drake.

Not long after most of Durin's Folk abandoned the Grey Mountains. Grór, Dáin's son, went away with many followers to the Iron Hills; but Thrór, Dáin's heir, with Borin his father's brother and the remainder of the people returned to Erebor. To the Great Hall of Thráin, Thrór brought back the Arkenstone, and he and his folk prospered and became rich, and they had the friendship of all Men that dwelt near. For they made not only things of wonder and beauty but weapons and armour of great worth; and there was great traffic of ore between them and their kin in the Iron Hills. Thus the Northmen who lived between Celduin (River Running) and Carnen (Redwater) became

[1] II, p. 135.
[2] Or released from prison; it may well be that it had already been awakened by the malice of Sauron.
[3] *The Hobbit*, p. 244.

strong and drove back all enemies from the East; and the Dwarves lived in plenty, and there was feasting and song in the Halls of Erebor.[1]

So the rumour of the wealth of Erebor spread abroad and reached the ears of the dragons, and at last Smaug the Golden, greatest of the dragons of his day, arose and without warning came against King Thrór and descended on the Mountain in flames. It was not long before all that realm was destroyed, and the town of Dale near by was ruined and deserted; but Smaug entered into the Great Hall and lay there upon a bed of gold.

From the sack and the burning many of Thrór's kin escaped; and last of all from the halls by a secret door came Thrór himself and his son Thráin II. They went away south with their family[2] into long and homeless wandering. With them went also a small company of their kinsmen and faithful followers.

Years afterwards Thrór, now old, poor, and desperate, gave to his son Thráin the one great treasure he still possessed, the last of the Seven Rings, and then he went away with one old companion only, called Nár. Of the Ring he said to Thráin at their parting:

'This may prove the foundation of new fortune for you yet, though that seems unlikely. But it needs gold to breed gold.'

'Surely you do not think of returning to Erebor?' said Thráin.

'Not at my age,' said Thrór. 'Our vengeance on Smaug I bequeath to you and your sons. But I am tired of poverty and the scorn of Men. I go to see what I can find.' He did not say where.

He was a little crazed perhaps with age and misfortune and long brooding on the splendour of Moria in his forefathers' days; or the Ring, it may be, was turning to evil now that its master was awake, driving him to folly and destruction. From Dunland,

---

[1] *The Hobbit*, p. 22.

[2] Among whom were the children of Thráin II: Thorin (Oakenshield), Frerin, and Dís. Thorin was then a youngster in the reckoning of the Dwarves. It was afterwards learned that more of the Folk under the Mountain had escaped than was at first hoped; but most of these went to the Iron Hills.

where he was then dwelling, he went north with Nár, and they crossed the Redhorn Pass and came down into Azanulbizar.

When Thrór came to Moria the Gate was open. Nár begged him to beware, but he took no heed of him, and walked proudly in as an heir that returns. But he did not come back. Nár stayed near by for many days in hiding. One day he heard a loud shout and the blare of a horn, and a body was flung out on the steps. Fearing that it was Thrór, he began to creep near, but there came a voice from within the gate:

'Come on, beardling! We can see you. But there is no need to be afraid today. We need you as a messenger.'

Then Nár came up, and found that it was indeed the body of Thrór, but the head was severed and lay face downwards. As he knelt there, he heard orc-laughter in the shadows, and the voice said:

'If beggars will not wait at the door, but sneak in to try thieving, that is what we do to them. If any of your people poke their foul beards in here again, they will fare the same. Go and tell them so! But if his family wish to know who is now king here, the name is written on his face. I wrote it! I killed him! I am the master!'

Then Nár turned the head and saw branded on the brow in Dwarf-runes so that he could read it the name AZOG. That name was branded in his heart and in the hearts of all the Dwarves afterwards. Nár stooped to take the head, but the voice of Azog[1] said:

'Drop it! Be off! Here's your fee, beggar-beard.' A small bag struck him. It held a few coins of little worth.

Weeping, Nár fled down the Silverlode; but he looked back once and saw that Orcs had come from the gate and were hacking up the body and flinging the pieces to the black crows.

Such was the tale that Nár brought back to Thráin; and when he had wept and torn his beard he fell silent. Seven days he sat and said no word. Then he stood up and said: 'This cannot be borne!' That was the beginning of the War of the Dwarves and

---

[1] Azog was the father of Bolg; see *The Hobbit*, p. 24.

the Orcs, which was long and deadly, and fought for the most part in deep places beneath the earth.

Thráin at once sent messengers bearing the tale, north, east, and west; but it was three years before the Dwarves had mustered their strength. Durin's Folk gathered all their host, and they were joined by great forces sent from the Houses of other Fathers; for this dishonour to the heir of the Eldest of their race filled them with wrath. When all was ready they assailed and sacked one by one all the strongholds of the Orcs that they could from Gundabad to the Gladden. Both sides were pitiless, and there was death and cruel deeds by dark and by light. But the Dwarves had the victory through their strength, and their matchless weapons, and the fire of their anger, as they hunted for Azog in every den under mountain.

At last all the Orcs that fled before them were gathered in Moria, and the Dwarf-host in pursuit came to Azanulbizar. That was a great vale that lay between the arms of the mountains about the lake of Kheled-zâram and had been of old part of the kingdom of Khazad-dûm. When the Dwarves saw the gate of their ancient mansions upon the hill-side they sent up a great shout like thunder in the valley. But a great host of foes was arrayed on the slopes above them, and out of the gates poured a multitude of Orcs that had been held back by Azog for the last need.

At first fortune was against the Dwarves; for it was a dark day of winter without sun, and the Orcs did not waver, and they outnumbered their enemies, and had the higher ground. So began the Battle of Azanulbizar (or Nanduhirion in the Elvish tongue), at the memory of which the Orcs still shudder and the Dwarves weep. The first assault of the vanguard led by Thráin was thrown back with loss, and Thráin was driven into a wood of great trees that then still grew not far from Kheled-zâram. There Frerin his son fell, and Fundin his kinsman, and many others, and both Thráin and Thorin were wounded.[1] Elsewhere the battle swayed to and fro with great slaughter, until at last the people of the Iron

---

[1] It is said that Thorin's shield was cloven and he cast it away and he hewed off with his axe a branch of an oak and held it in his left hand to ward off the strokes of his foes, or to wield as a club. In this way he got his name.

Hills turned the day. Coming late and fresh to the field the mailed warriors of Náin, Grór's son, drove through the Orcs to the very threshold of Moria, crying 'Azog! Azog!' as they hewed down with their mattocks all who stood in their way.

Then Náin stood before the Gate and cried with a great voice: 'Azog! If you are in come out! Or is the play in the valley too rough?'

Thereupon Azog came forth, and he was a great Orc with a huge iron-clad head, and yet agile and strong. With him came many like him, the fighters of his guard, and as they engaged Náin's company he turned to Náin, and said:

'What? Yet another beggar at my doors? Must I brand you too?' With that he rushed at Náin and they fought. But Náin was half blind with rage, and also very weary with battle, whereas Azog was fresh and fell and full of guile. Soon Náin made a great stroke with all his strength that remained, but Azog darted aside and kicked Náin's leg, so that the mattock splintered on the stone where he had stood, but Náin stumbled forward. Then Azog with a swift swing hewed his neck. His mail-collar withstood the edge, but so heavy was the blow that Náin's neck was broken and he fell.

Then Azog laughed, and he lifted up his head to let forth a great yell of triumph; but the cry died in his throat. For he saw that all his host in the valley was in a rout, and the Dwarves went this way and that slaying as they would, and those that could escape from them were flying south, shrieking as they ran. And hard by all the soldiers of his guard lay dead. He turned and fled back towards the Gate.

Up the steps after him leaped a Dwarf with a red axe. It was Dáin Ironfoot, Náin's son. Right before the doors he caught Azog, and there he slew him, and hewed off his head. That was held a great feat, for Dáin was then only a stripling in the reckoning of the Dwarves. But long life and many battles lay before him, until old but unbowed he fell at last in the War of the Ring. Yet hardy and full of wrath as he was, it is said that when he came down from the Gate he looked grey in the face, as one who has felt great fear.

When at last the battle was won the Dwarves that were left

gathered in Azanulbizar. They took the head of Azog and thrust into its mouth the purse of small money, and then they set it on a stake. But no feast nor song was there that night; for their dead were beyond the count of grief. Barely half of their number, it is said, could still stand or had hope of healing.

None the less in the morning Thráin stood before them. He had one eye blinded beyond cure, and he was halt with a leg-wound; but he said: 'Good! We have the victory. Khazad-dûm is ours!'

But they answered: 'Durin's Heir you may be, but even with one eye you should see clearer. We fought this war for vengeance, and vengeance we have taken. But it is not sweet. If this is victory, then our hands are too small to hold it.'

And those who were not of Durin's Folk said also: 'Khazad-dûm was not our Fathers' house. What is it to us, unless a hope of treasure? But now, if we must go without the rewards and the weregilds that are owed to us, the sooner we return to our own lands the better pleased we shall be.'

Then Thráin turned to Dáin, and said: 'But surely my own kin will not desert me?' 'No,' said Dáin. 'You are the father of our Folk, and we have bled for you, and will again. But we will not enter Khazad-dûm. You will not enter Khazad-dûm. Only I have looked through the shadow of the Gate. Beyond the shadow it waits for you still: Durin's Bane. The world must change and some other power than ours must come before Durin's Folk walk again in Moria.'

So it was that after Azanulbizar the Dwarves dispersed again. But first with great labour they stripped all their dead, so that Orcs should not come and win there a store of weapons and mail. It is said that every Dwarf that went from that battlefield was bowed under a heavy burden. Then they built many pyres and burned all the bodies of their kin. There was a great felling of trees in the valley, which remained bare ever after, and the reek of the burning was seen in Lórien.[1]

---

[1] Such dealings with their dead seemed grievous to the Dwarves, for it was against their use; but to make such tombs as they were accustomed to build (since they will lay their dead only in stone not in earth) would have taken many years. To fire therefore they turned, rather than leave their kin to beast or bird or carrion-orc. But those who fell in Azanulbizar

When the dreadful fires were in ashes the allies went away to their own countries, and Dáin Ironfoot led his father's people back to the Iron Hills. Then standing by the great stake, Thráin said to Thorin Oakenshield: 'Some would think this head dearly bought! At least we have given our kingdom for it. Will you come with me back to the anvil? Or will you beg your bread at proud doors?'

'To the anvil,' answered Thorin. 'The hammer will at least keep the arms strong, until they can wield sharper tools again.'

So Thráin and Thorin with what remained of their following (among whom were Balin and Glóin) returned to Dunland, and soon afterwards they removed and wandered in Eriador, until at last they made a home in exile in the east of the Ered Luin beyond the Lune. Of iron were most of the things that they forged in those days, but they prospered after a fashion, and their numbers slowly increased.[1] But, as Thrór had said, the Ring needed gold to breed gold, and of that or any other precious metal they had little or none.

Of this Ring something may be said here. It was believed by the Dwarves of Durin's Folk to be the first of the Seven that was forged; and they say that it was given to the King of Khazad-dûm, Durin III, by the Elven-smiths themselves and not by Sauron, though doubtless his evil power was on it, since he had aided in the forging of all the Seven. But the possessors of the Ring did not display it or speak of it, and they seldom surrendered it until near death, so that others did not know for certain where it was bestowed. Some thought that it had remained in Khazad-dûm, in the secret tombs of the kings, if they had not been discovered and plundered; but among the kindred of Durin's Heir it was believed (wrongly) that Thrór had worn it when he rashly returned there. What then had become of it they did not know. It was not found on the body of Azog.[2]

---

were honoured in memory, and to this day a Dwarf will say proudly of one of his sires: 'he was a burned Dwarf', and that is enough.

[1] They had very few women-folk. Dís Thráin's daughter was there. She was the mother of Fíli and Kíli, who were born in the Ered Luin. Thorin had no wife.

[2] II, p. 70.

None the less it may well be, as the Dwarves now believe, that Sauron by his arts had discovered who had this Ring, the last to remain free, and that the singular misfortunes of the heirs of Durin were largely due to his malice. For the Dwarves had proved untameable by this means. The only power over them that the Rings wielded was to inflame their hearts with a greed of gold and precious things, so that if they lacked them all other good things seemed profitless, and they were filled with wrath and desire for vengeance on all who deprived them. But they were made from their beginning of a kind to resist most steadfastly any domination. Though they could be slain or broken, they could not be reduced to shadows enslaved to another will; and for the same reason their lives were not affected by any Ring, to live either longer or shorter because of it. All the more did Sauron hate the possessors and desire to dispossess them.

It was therefore perhaps partly by the malice of the Ring that Thráin after some years became restless and discontented. The lust for gold was ever in his mind. At last, when he could endure it no longer, he turned his thoughts to Erebor, and resolved to go back there. He said nothing to Thorin of what was in his heart; but with Balin and Dwalin and a few others, he arose and said farewell and departed.

Little is known of what happened to him afterwards. It would now seem that as soon as he was abroad with few companions he was hunted by the emissaries of Sauron. Wolves pursued him, Orcs waylaid him, evil birds shadowed his path, and the more he strove to go north the more misfortunes opposed him. There came a dark night when he and his companions were wandering in the land beyond Anduin, and they were driven by a black rain to take shelter under the eaves of Mirkwood. In the morning he was gone from the camp, and his companions called him in vain. They searched for him many days, until at last giving up hope they departed and came at length back to Thorin. Only long after was it learned that Thráin had been taken alive and brought to the pits of Dol Guldur. There he was tormented and the Ring taken from him, and there at last he died.

So Thorin Oakenshield became the Heir of Durin, but an heir

without hope. When Thráin was lost he was ninety-five, a great dwarf of proud bearing; but he seemed content to remain in Eriador. There he laboured long, and trafficked, and gained such wealth as he could; and his people were increased by many of the wandering Folk of Durin who heard of his dwelling in the west and came to him. Now they had fair halls in the mountains, and store of goods, and their days did not seem so hard, though in their songs they spoke ever of the Lonely Mountain far away.

The years lengthened. The embers in the heart of Thorin grew hot again, as he brooded on the wrongs of his House and the vengeance upon the Dragon that he had inherited. He thought of weapons and armies and alliances, as his great hammer rang in his forge; but the armies were dispersed and the alliances broken and the axes of his people were few; and a great anger without hope burned him as he smote the red iron on the anvil.

But at last there came about by chance a meeting between Gandalf and Thorin that changed all the fortunes of the House of Durin, and led to other and greater ends beside. On a time[1] Thorin, returning west from a journey, stayed at Bree for the night. There Gandalf was also. He was on his way to the Shire, which he had not visited for some twenty years. He was weary, and thought to rest there for a while.

Among many cares he was troubled in mind by the perilous state of the North; because he knew then already that Sauron was plotting war, and intended, as soon as he felt strong enough, to attack Rivendell. But to resist any attempt from the East to regain the lands of Angmar and the northern passes in the mountains there were now only the Dwarves of the Iron Hills. And beyond them lay the desolation of the Dragon. The Dragon Sauron might use with terrible effect. How then could the end of Smaug be achieved?

It was even as Gandalf sat and pondered this that Thorin stood before him, and said: 'Master Gandalf, I know you only by sight, but now I should be glad to speak with you. For you

[1] March 15, 2941.

have often come into my thoughts of late, as if I were bidden
to seek you. Indeed I should have done so, if I had known where
to find you.'

Gandalf looked at him with wonder. 'That is strange, Thorin
Oakenshield,' he said. 'For I have thought of you also; and
though I am on my way to the Shire, it was in my mind that is
the way also to your halls.'

'Call them so, if you will,' said Thorin. 'They are only poor
lodgings in exile. But you would be welcome there, if you would
come. For they say that you are wise and know more than any
other of what goes on in the world; and I have much on my
mind and would be glad of your counsel.'

'I will come,' said Gandalf; 'for I guess that we share one
trouble at least. The Dragon of Erebor is on my mind, and I do
not think that he will be forgotten by the grandson of Thrór.'

The story is told elsewhere of what came of that meeting: of the
strange plan that Gandalf made for the help of Thorin, and how
Thorin and his companions set out from the Shire on the quest
of the Lonely Mountain that came to great ends unforeseen.
Here only those things are recalled that directly concern Durin's
Folk.

The Dragon was slain by Bard of Esgaroth, but there was
battle in Dale. For the Orcs came down upon Erebor as soon
as they heard of the return of the Dwarves; and they were led
by Bolg, son of that Azog whom Dáin slew in his youth. In that
first Battle of Dale, Thorin Oakenshield was mortally wounded;
and he died and was laid in a tomb under the Mountain with
the Arkenstone upon his breast. There fell also Fíli and Kíli, his
sister-sons. But Dáin Ironfoot, his cousin, who came from the
Iron Hills to his aid and was also his rightful heir, became then
King Dáin II, and the Kingdom under the Mountain was
restored, even as Gandalf had desired. Dáin proved a great and
wise king, and the Dwarves prospered and grew strong again in
his day.

In the late summer of that same year (2941) Gandalf had at
last prevailed upon Saruman and the White Council to attack
Dol Guldur, and Sauron retreated and went to Mordor, there
to be secure, as he thought, from all his enemies. So it was

that when the War came at last the main assault was turned southwards; yet even so with his far-stretched right hand Sauron might have done great evil in the North, if King Dáin and King Brand had not stood in his path. Even as Gandalf said afterwards to Frodo and Gimli, when they dwelt together for a time in Minas Tirith. Not long before news had come to Gondor of events far away.

'I grieved at the fall of Thorin,' said Gandalf; 'and now we hear that Dáin has fallen, fighting in Dale again, even while we fought here. I should call that a heavy loss, if it was not a wonder rather that in his great age he could still wield his axe as mightily as they say that he did, standing over the body of King Brand before the Gate of Erebor until the darkness fell.

'Yet things might have gone far otherwise and far worse. When you think of the great Battle of the Pelennor, do not forget the battles in Dale and the valour of Durin's Folk. Think of what might have been. Dragon-fire and savage swords in Eriador, night in Rivendell. There might be no Queen in Gondor. We might now hope to return from the victory here only to ruin and ash. But that has been averted – because I met Thorin Oakenshield one evening on the edge of spring in Bree. A chance-meeting, as we say in Middle-earth.'

Dís was the daughter of Thráin II. She is the only dwarf-woman named in these histories. It was said by Gimli that there are few dwarf-women, probably no more than a third of the whole people. They seldom walk abroad except at great need. They are in voice and appearance, and in garb if they must go on a journey, so like to the dwarf-men that the eyes and ears of other peoples cannot tell them apart. This has given rise to the foolish opinion among Men that there are no dwarf-women, and that the Dwarves 'grow out of stone'.

It is because of the fewness of women among them that the kind of the Dwarves increases slowly, and is in peril when they have no secure dwellings. For Dwarves take only one wife or husband each in their lives, and are jealous, as in all matters of their rights. The number of dwarf-men that marry is actually less than one-third. For not all the women take husbands: some desire none; some desire one that they cannot get, and so will

The Line of the Dwarves of Erebor as it was set out by Gimli Glóin's son for King Elessar.

Durin the Deathless
(First Age)
|
*Durin VI
1731–1980†
|
*Náin I
1832–1981†
|
*Thráin I
1934–2190
|
*Thorin I
2035–2289
|
*Glóin
2136–2385
|
*Óin
2238–2488
|
*Náin II
2338–2585

*Dáin I
2440–2589†

Borin
2450–2711
|
Farin
2560–2803

*Thrór
2542–2790†
|
*Thráin II
2644–2850†

Frór
2552–2589†

Grór
2563–2805
|
Náin
2665–2799†
|
*Dáin II
Ironfoot
2767–3019†
|
*Thorin III
Stonehelm
2866
⋮
(Durin VII
& Last)

Fundin
2662–2799†

Gróin
2671–2923

*Thorin II
Oakenshield
2746–2941†

Frerin
2751–
2799†

Dís
2760

Fíli
2859–
2941†

Kíli
2864–
2941†

Balin
2763–
2994†

Dwalin
2772–
3112

Óin
2774–
2994†

Glóin
2783–
F.A. 15
|
Gimli
Elf-friend
2879–3141
(F.A. 120)

Foundation of Erebor, 1999.
Dáin I slain by a dragon, 2589
Return to Erebor, 2590.
Sack of Erebor, 2770.
Murder of Thrór, 2790.
Mustering of the Dwarves, 2790–3.
War of the Dwarves and Orcs, 2793–9.

Battle of Nanduhirion, 2799.
Thráin goes wandering, 2841.
Death of Thráin and loss of his Ring, 2850.
Battle of Five Armies and death of Thorin II, 2941.
Balin goes to Moria, 2989.

* The names of those who were held to be kings of Durin's Folk, whether in exile or not, are marked so. Of the other companions of Thorin Oakenshield in the journey to Erebor Ori, Nori, and Dori were also of the House of Durin, and more remote kinsmen of Thorin: Bifur, Bofur, and Bombur were descended from Dwarves of Moria but were not of Durin's line. For † see III, p. 379.

have no other. As for the men, very many also do not desire marriage, being engrossed in their crafts.

Gimli Glóin's son is renowned, for he was one of the Nine Walkers that set out with the Ring; and he remained in the company of King Elessar throughout the War. He was named Elf-friend because of the great love that grew between him and Legolas, son of King Thranduil, and because of his reverence for the Lady Galadriel.

After the fall of Sauron, Gimli brought south a part of the Dwarf-folk of Erebor, and he became Lord of the Glittering Caves. He and his people did great works in Gondor and Rohan. For Minas Tirith they forged gates of *mithril* and steel to replace those broken by the Witch-king. Legolas his friend also brought south Elves out of Greenwood, and they dwelt in Ithilien, and it became once again the fairest country in all the westlands.

But when King Elessar gave up his life Legolas followed at last the desire of his heart and sailed over Sea.

Here follows one of the last notes in the Red Book

We have heard tell that Legolas took Gimli Glóin's son with him because of their great friendship, greater than any that has been between Elf and Dwarf. If this is true, then it is strange indeed: that a Dwarf should be willing to leave Middle-earth for any love, or that the Eldar should receive him, or that the Lords of the West should permit it. But it is said that Gimli went also out of desire to see again the beauty of Galadriel; and it may be that she, being mighty among the Eldar, obtained this grace for him. More cannot be said of this matter.

APPENDIX B

THE TALE OF YEARS

(CHRONOLOGY OF THE WESTLANDS)

The *First Age* ended with the Great Battle, in which the Host of Valinor broke Thangorodrim[1] and overthrew Morgoth. Then most of the Noldor returned into the Far West[2] and dwelt in Eressëa within sight of Valinor; and many of the Sindar went over Sea also.

The *Second Age* ended with the first overthrow of Sauron, servant of Morgoth, and the taking of the One Ring.

The *Third Age* came to its end in the War of the Ring; but the *Fourth Age* was not held to have begun until Master Elrond departed, and the time was come for the dominion of Men and the decline of all other 'speaking-peoples' in Middle-earth.[3]

In the Fourth Age the earlier ages were often called the *Elder Days*; but that name was properly given only to the days before the casting out of Morgoth. The histories of that time are not recorded here.

The Second Age

These were the dark years for Men of Middle-earth, but the years of the glory of Númenor. Of events in Middle-earth the records are few and brief, and their dates are often uncertain.

In the beginning of this age many of the High Elves still remained. Most of these dwelt in Lindon west of the Ered Luin; but before the building of the Barad-dûr many of the Sindar passed eastward, and some established realms in the forests far away, where their people were mostly Silvan Elves. Thranduil, king in the north of Greenwood the Great, was one of these. In Lindon north of the Lune dwelt Gil-galad, last heir of the kings of the Noldor in exile. He was acknowledged as High King of

[1] II, p. 36.
[2] III, p. 248, *The Hobbit*, p. 151.
[3] VI, p. 104.

the Elves of the West. In Lindon south of the Lune dwelt for a time Celeborn, kinsman of Thingol; his wife was Galadriel, greatest of Elven women. She was sister of Finrod Felagund, Friend-of-Men, once king of Nargothrond, who gave his life to save Beren son of Barahir.

Later some of the Noldor went to Eregion, upon the west of the Misty Mountains, and near to the West-gate of Moria. This they did because they learned that *mithril* had been discovered in Moria.[1] The Noldor were great craftsmen and less unfriendly to the Dwarves than the Sindar; but the friendship that grew up between the people of Durin and the Elven-smiths of Eregion was the closest that there has ever been between the two races. Celebrimbor was Lord of Eregion and the greatest of their crafts-men; he was descended from Fëanor.

Year
1 Foundation of the Grey Havens, and of Lindon.
32 The Edain reach Númenor.
c. 40 Many Dwarves leaving their old cities in Ered Luin go to Moria and swell its numbers.
442 Death of Elros Tar-Minyatur.
c. 500 Sauron begins to stir again in Middle-earth.
548 Birth in Númenor of Silmariën.
600 The first ships of the Númenoreans appear off the coasts.
750 Eregion founded by the Noldor.
c. 1000 Sauron, alarmed by the growing power of the Númenoreans, chooses Mordor as a land to make into a stronghold. He begins the building of Barad-dûr.
1075 Tar-Ancalimë becomes the first Ruling Queen of Númenor.
1200 Sauron endeavours to seduce the Eldar. Gil-galad refuses to treat with him; but the smiths of Eregion are won over. The Númenoreans begin to make per-manent havens.
c. 1500 The Elven-smiths instructed by Sauron reach the height of their skill. They begin the forging of the Rings of Power.

[1] II, p. 135.

c. 1590   The Three Rings are completed in Eregion.

c. 1600   Sauron forges the One Ring in Orodruin. He completes the Barad-dûr. Celebrimbor perceives the designs of Sauron.

1693   War of the Elves and Sauron begins. The Three Rings are hidden.

1695   Sauron's forces invade Eriador. Gil-galad sends Elrond to Eregion.

1697   Eregion laid waste. Death of Celebrimbor. The gates of Moria are shut. Elrond retreats with remnant of the Noldor and founds the refuge of Imladris.

1699   Sauron overruns Eriador.

1700   Tar-Minastir sends a great navy from Númenor to Lindon. Sauron is defeated.

1701   Sauron is driven out of Eriador. The Westlands have peace for a long while.

c. 1800   From about this time onward the Númenoreans begin to establish dominions on the coasts. Sauron extends his power eastwards. The shadow falls on Númenor.

2251   Tar-Atanamir takes the sceptre. Rebellion and division of the Númenoreans begins. About this time the Nazgûl or Ringwraiths, slaves of the Nine Rings, first appear.

2280   Umbar is made into a great fortress of Númenor.

2350   Pelargir is built. It becomes the chief haven of the Faithful Númenoreans.

2899   Ar-Adûnakhôr takes the sceptre.

3175   Repentance of Tar-Palantir. Civil war in Númenor.

3255   Ar-Pharazôn the Golden seizes the sceptre.

3261   Ar-Pharazôn sets sail and lands at Umbar.

3262   Sauron is taken as prisoner to Númenor; 3262–3310 Sauron seduces the King and corrupts the Númenoreans.

3310   Ar-Pharazôn begins the building of the Great Armament.

3319   Ar-Pharazôn assails Valinor. Downfall of Númenor. Elendil and his sons escape.

3320   Foundations of the Realms in Exile: Arnor and Gondor. The Stones are divided (II, p. 248). Sauron returns to Mordor.

3429 Sauron attacks Gondor, takes Minas Ithil and burns
the White Tree. Isildur escapes down Anduin and
goes to Elendil in the North. Anárion defends Minas
Anor and Osgiliath.

3430 The Last Alliance of Elves and Men is formed.

3431 Gil-galad and Elendil march east to Imladris.

3434 The host of the Alliance crosses the Misty Mountains.
Battle of Dagorlad and defeat of Sauron. Siege of
Barad-dûr begins.

3440 Anárion slain.

3441 Sauron overthrown by Elendil and Gil-galad, who
perish. Isildur takes the One Ring. Sauron passes
away and the Ringwraiths go into the shadows. The
Second Age ends.

The Third Age

These were the fading years of the Eldar. For long they were at
peace, wielding the Three Rings while Sauron slept and the One
Ring was lost; but they attempted nothing new, living in memory
of the past. The Dwarves hid themselves in deep places,
guarding their hoards; but when evil began to stir again and
dragons reappeared, one by one their ancient treasures were
plundered, and they became a wandering people. Moria for long
remained secure, but its numbers dwindled until many of its
vast mansions became dark and empty. The wisdom and the
life-span of the Númenoreans also waned as they became
mingled with lesser Men.

When maybe a thousand years had passed, and the first
shadow had fallen on Greenwood the Great, the *Istari* or Wizards
appeared in Middle-earth. It was afterwards said that they came
out of the Far West and were messengers sent to contest the
power of Sauron, and to unite all those who had the will to resist
him; but they were forbidden to match his power with power,
or to seek to dominate Elves or Men by force and fear.

They came therefore in the shape of Men, though they were
never young and aged only slowly, and they had many powers
of mind and hand. They revealed their true names to few,[1] but

---

[1] IV, p. 94.

used such names as were given to them. The two highest of this order (of whom it is said there were five) were called by the Eldar Curunír, 'the Man of Skill', and Mithrandir, 'the Grey Pilgrim', but by Men in the North Saruman and Gandalf. Curunír journeyed often into the East, but dwelt at last in Isengard. Mithrandir was closest in friendship with the Eldar, and wandered mostly in the West and never made for himself any lasting abode.

Throughout the Third Age the guardianship of the Three Rings was known only to those who possessed them. But at the end it became known that they had been held at first by the three greatest of the Eldar: Gil-galad, Galadriel and Círdan. Gil-galad before he died gave his ring to Elrond; Círdan later surrendered his to Mithrandir. For Círdan saw further and deeper than any other in Middle-earth, and he welcomed Mithrandir at the Grey Havens, knowing whence he came and whither he would return.

'Take this ring, Master,' he said, 'for your labours will be heavy; but it will support you in the weariness that you have taken upon yourself. For this is the Ring of Fire, and with it you may rekindle hearts in a world that grows chill. But as for me, my heart is with the Sea, and I will dwell by the grey shores until the last ship sails. I will await you.'

Year

   2 Isildur plants a seedling of the White Tree in Minas Anor. He delivers the South-kingdom to Meneldil. Disaster of the Gladden Fields; Isildur and his three elder sons are slain.

   3 Ohtar brings the shards of Narsil to Imladris.

  10 Valandil becomes King of Arnor.

109 Elrond weds Celebrían, daughter of Celeborn.

130 Birth of Elladan and Elrohir, sons of Elrond.

241 Birth of Arwen Undómiel.

420 King Ostoher rebuilds Minas Anor.

490 First invasion of Easterlings.

500 Rómendacil I defeats the Easterlings.

541 Rómendacil slain in battle.

830 Falastur begins the line of the Ship-kings of Gondor.

861 Death of Eärendur, and division of Arnor.

933 King Eärnil I takes Umbar, which becomes a fortress of Gondor.

936 Eärnil lost at sea.

1015 King Ciryandil slain in the siege of Umbar.

1050 Hyarmendacil conquers the Harad. Gondor reaches the height of its power. About this time a shadow falls on Greenwood, and men begin to call it Mirkwood. The Periannath are first mentioned in records, with the coming of the Harfoots to Eriador.

c. 1100 The Wise (the Istari and the chief Eldar) discover that an evil power has made a stronghold at Dol Guldur. It is thought to be one of the Nazgûl.

1149 Reign of Atanatar Alcarin begins.

c. 1150 The Fallohides enter Eriador. The Stoors come over the Redhorn Pass and move to the Angle, or to Dunland.

c. 1300 Evil things begin to multiply again. Orcs increase in the Misty Mountains and attack the Dwarves. The Nazgûl reappear. The chief of these comes north to Angmar. The Periannath migrate westward; many settle at Bree.

1356 King Argeleb I slain in battle with Rhudaur. About this time the Stoors leave the Angle, and some return to Wilderland.

1409 The Witch-king of Angmar invades Arnor. King Arveleg I slain. Fornost and Tyrn Gorthad are defended. The Tower of Amon Sûl destroyed.

1432 King Valacar of Gondor dies, and the civil war of the Kin-strife begins.

1437 Burning of Osgiliath and loss of the *palantír*. Eldacar flees to Rhovanion; his son Ornendil is murdered.

1447 Eldacar returns and drives out the usurper Castamir. Battle of the Crossings of Erui. Siege of Pelargir.

1448 Rebels escape and seize Umbar.

1540 King Aldamir slain in war with the Harad and Corsairs of Umbar.

1551 Hyarmendacil II defeats the Men of Harad.

1601 Many Periannath migrate from Bree, and are granted land beyond Baranduin by Argeleb II.

c. 1630 They are joined by Stoors coming up from Dunland.

1634 The Corsairs ravage Pelargir and slay King Minardil.

1636 The Great Plague devastates Gondor. Death of King Telemnar and his children. The White Tree dies in Minas Anor. The plague spreads north and west, and many parts of Eriador become desolate. Beyond the Baranduin the Periannath survive, but suffer great loss.

1640 King Tarondor removes the King's House to Minas Anor, and plants a seedling of the White Tree. Osgiliath begins to fall into ruin. Mordor is left unguarded.

1810 King Telumehtar Umbardacil retakes Umbar and drives out the Corsairs.

1851 The attacks of the Wainriders upon Gondor begin.

1856 Gondor loses its eastern territories, and Narmacil II falls in battle.

1899 King Calimehtar defeats the Wainriders on Dagorlad.

1900 Calimehtar builds the White Tower in Minas Anor.

1940 Gondor and Arnor renew communications and form an alliance. Arvedui weds Fíriel daughter of Ondoher of Gondor.

1944 Ondoher falls in battle. Eärnil defeats the enemy in South Ithilien. He then wins the Battle of the Camp, and drives Wainriders into the Dead Marshes. Arvedui claims the crown of Gondor.

1945 Eärnil II receives the crown.

1974 End of the North-kingdom. The Witch-king overruns Arthedain and takes Fornost.

1975 Arvedui drowned in the Bay of Forochel. The *palantíri* of Annúminas and Amon Sûl are lost. Eärnur brings a fleet to Lindon. The Witch-king defeated at the Battle of Fornost, and pursued to the Ettenmoors. He vanishes from the North.

1976 Aranarth takes the title of Chieftain of the Dúnedain. The heirlooms of Arnor are given into the keeping of Elrond.

1977 Frumgar leads the Éothéod into the North.

1979 Bucca of the Marish becomes first Thain of the Shire.

1980 The Witch-king comes to Mordor and there gathers

the Nazgûl. A Balrog appears in Moria, and slays Durin VI.

1981　Náin I slain. The Dwarves flee from Moria. Many of the Silvan Elves of Lórien flee south. Amroth and Nimrodel are lost.

1999　Thráin I comes to Erebor and founds a dwarf-kingdom 'under the Mountain'.

2000　The Nazgûl issue from Mordor and besiege Minas Ithil.

2002　Fall of Minas Ithil, afterwards known as Minas Morgul. The *palantír* is captured.

2043　Eärnur becomes King of Gondor. He is challenged by the Witch-king.

2050　The challenge is renewed. Eärnur rides to Minas Morgul and is lost. Mardil becomes the first Ruling Steward.

2060　The power of Dol Guldur grows. The Wise fear that it may be Sauron taking shape again.

2063　Gandalf goes to Dol Guldur. Sauron retreats and hides in the East. The Watchful Peace begins. The Nazgûl remain quiet in Minas Morgul.

2210　Thorin I leaves Erebor, and goes north to the Grey Mountains, where most of the remnants of Durin's Folk are now gathering.

2340　Isumbras I becomes thirteenth Thain, and first of the Took line. The Oldbucks occupy the Buckland.

2460　The Watchful Peace ends. Sauron returns with increased strength to Dol Guldur.

2463　The White Council is formed. About this time Déagol the Stoor finds the One Ring, and is murdered by Sméagol.

2470　About this time Sméagol-Gollum hides in the Misty Mountains.

2475　Attack on Gondor renewed. Osgiliath finally ruined, and its stone-bridge broken.

c. 2480　Orcs begin to make secret strongholds in the Misty Mountains so as to bar all the passes into Eriador. Sauron begins to people Moria with his creatures.

2509　Celebrían, journeying to Lórien, is waylaid in the

Redhorn Pass, and receives a poisoned wound.

2510 Celebrían departs over Sea. Orcs and Easterlings overrun Calenardhon. Eorl the Young wins the victory of the Field of Celebrant. The Rohirrim settle in Calenardhon.

2545 Eorl falls in battle in the Wold.

2569 Brego son of Eorl completes the Golden Hall.

2570 Baldor son of Brego enters the Forbidden Door and is lost. About this time Dragons reappear in the far North and begin to afflict the Dwarves.

2589 Dáin I slain by a Dragon.

2590 Thrór returns to Erebor. Grór his brother goes to the Iron Hills.

c. 2670 Tobold plants 'pipe-weed' in the Southfarthing.

2683 Isengrim II becomes tenth Thain and begins the excavation of Great Smials.

2698 Ecthelion I rebuilds the White Tower in Minas Tirith.

2740 Orcs renew their invasions of Eriador.

2747 Bandobras Took defeats an Orc-band in the North-farthing.

2758 Rohan attacked from west and east and overrun. Gondor attacked by fleets of the Corsairs. Helm of Rohan takes refuge in Helm's Deep. Wulf seizes Edoras. 2758–9: The Long Winter follows. Great suffering and loss of life in Eriador and Rohan. Gandalf comes to the aid of the Shire-folk.

2759 Death of Helm. Fréaláf drives out Wulf, and begins second line of Kings of the Mark. Saruman takes up his abode in Isengard.

2770 Smaug the Dragon descends on Erebor. Dale destroyed. Thrór escapes with Thráin II and Thorin II.

2790 Thrór slain by an Orc in Moria. The Dwarves gather for a war of vengeance. Birth of Gerontius, later known as the Old Took.

2793 The War of the Dwarves and Orcs begins.

2799 Battle of Nanduhirion before the East-gate of Moria. Dáin Ironfoot returns to the Iron Hills. Thráin II and his son Thorin wander westwards. They settle in the

South of Ered Luin beyond the Shire (2802).

2800–64 Orcs from the North trouble Rohan. King Walda slain by them (2861).

2841 Thráin II sets out to revisit Erebor, but is pursued by the servants of Sauron.

2845 Thráin the Dwarf is imprisoned in Dol Guldur; the last of the Seven Rings is taken from him.

2850 Gandalf again enters Dol Guldur, and discovers that its master is indeed Sauron, who is gathering all the Rings and seeking for news of the One, and of Isildur's Heir. He finds Thráin and receives the key of Erebor. Thráin dies in Dol Guldur.

2851 The White Council meets. Gandalf urges an attack on Dol Guldur. Saruman overrules him.[1] Saruman begins to search near the Gladden Fields.

2852 Belecthor II of Gondor dies. The White Tree dies, and no seedling can be found. The Dead Tree is left standing.

2885 Stirred up by emissaries of Sauron the Haradrim cross the Poros and attack Gondor. The sons of Folcwine of Rohan are slain in the service of Gondor.

2890 Bilbo born in the Shire.

2901 Most of the remaining inhabitants of Ithilien desert it owing to the attacks of Uruks of Mordor. The secret refuge of Henneth Annûn is built.

2907 Birth of Gilraen mother of Aragorn II.

2911 The Fell Winter. The Baranduin and other rivers are frozen. White Wolves invade Eriador from the North.

2912 Great floods devastate Enedwaith and Minhiriath. Tharbad is ruined and deserted.

2920 Death of the Old Took.

2929 Arathorn son of Arador of the Dúnedain weds Gilraen.

2930 Arador slain by Trolls. Birth of Denethor II son of Ecthelion II in Minas Tirith.

---

[1] It afterwards became clear that Saruman had then begun to desire to possess the One Ring himself, and he hoped that it might reveal itself, seeking its master, if Sauron were let be for a time.

2931 Aragorn son of Arathorn II born on March 1st.

2933 Arathorn II slain. Gilraen takes Aragorn to Imladris. Elrond receives him as foster-son and gives him the name Estel (Hope); his ancestry is concealed.

2939 Saruman discovers that Sauron's servants are search-ing the Anduin near Gladden Fields, and that Sauron therefore has learned of Isildur's end. He is alarmed, but says nothing to the Council.

2941 Thorin Oakenshield and Gandalf visit Bilbo in the Shire. Bilbo meets Sméagol-Gollum and finds the Ring. The White Council meets; Saruman agrees to an attack on Dol Guldur, since he now wishes to pre-vent Sauron from searching the River. Sauron having made his plans abandons Dol Guldur. The Battle of the Five Armies in Dale. Death of Thorin II. Bard of Esgaroth slays Smaug. Dáin of the Iron Hills becomes King under the Mountain (Dáin II).

2942 Bilbo returns to the Shire with the Ring. Sauron returns in secret to Mordor.

2944 Bard rebuilds Dale and becomes King. Gollum leaves the Mountains and begins his search for the 'thief' of the Ring.

2948 Théoden son of Thengel, King of Rohan, born.

2949 Gandalf and Balin visit Bilbo in the Shire.

2950 Finduilas, daughter of Adrahil of Dol Amroth, born.

2951 Sauron declares himself openly and gathers power in Mordor. He begins the rebuilding of Barad-dûr. Gollum turns towards Mordor. Sauron sends three of the Nazgûl to reoccupy Dol Guldur.

Elrond reveals to 'Estel' his true name and ancestry, and delivers to him the shards of Narsil. Arwen, newly returned from Lórien, meets Aragorn in the woods of Imladris. Aragorn goes out into the Wild.

2953 Last meeting of the White Council. They debate the Rings. Saruman feigns that he has discovered that the One Ring has passed down Anduin to the Sea. Saruman withdraws to Isengard, which he takes as his own, and fortifies it. Being jealous and afraid of Gandalf he sets spies to watch all his movements; and notes his interest in the Shire. He soon begins to keep agents in Bree and the Southfarthing.

2954   Mount Doom bursts into flame again. The last inhabitants of Ithilien flee over Anduin.

2956   Aragorn meets Gandalf and their friendship begins.

2957–80   Aragorn undertakes his great journeys and errantries. As Thorongil he serves in disguise both Thengel of Rohan and Ecthelion II of Gondor.

2968   Birth of Frodo.

2976   Denethor weds Finduilas of Dol Amroth.

2977   Bain son of Bard becomes King of Dale.

2978   Birth of Boromir son of Denethor II.

2980   Aragorn enters Lórien, and there meets again Arwen Undómiel. Aragorn gives her the ring of Barahir, and they plight their troth upon the hill of Cerin Amroth. About this time Gollum reaches the confines of Mordor and becomes acquainted with Shelob. Théoden becomes King of Rohan.

2983   Faramir son of Denethor born. Birth of Samwise.

2984   Death of Ecthelion II. Denethor II becomes Steward of Gondor.

2988   Finduilas dies young.

2989   Balin leaves Erebor and enters Moria.

2991   Éomer Éomund's son born in Rohan.

2994   Balin perishes, and the dwarf-colony is destroyed.

2995   Éowyn sister of Éomer born.

c. 3000   The shadow of Mordor lengthens. Saruman dares to use the *palantír* of Orthanc, but becomes ensnared by Sauron, who has the Ithil Stone. He becomes a traitor to the Council. His spies report that the Shire is being closely guarded by the Rangers.

3001   Bilbo's farewell feast. Gandalf suspects his ring to be the One Ring. The guard on the Shire is doubled. Gandalf seeks for news of Gollum and calls on the help of Aragorn.

3002   Bilbo becomes a guest of Elrond, and settles in Rivendell.

3004   Gandalf visits Frodo in the Shire, and does so at intervals during the next four years.

3007 Brand son of Bain becomes King in Dale. Death of Gilraen.

3008 In the autumn Gandalf pays his last visit to Frodo.

3009 Gandalf and Aragorn renew their hunt for Gollum at intervals during the next eight years, searching in the vales of Anduin, Mirkwood, and Rhovanion to the confines of Mordor. At some time during these years Gollum himself ventured into Mordor, and was captured by Sauron. Elrond sends for Arwen, and she returns to Imladris; the Mountains and all lands eastward are becoming dangerous.

3017 Gollum is released from Mordor. He is taken by Aragorn in the Dead Marshes, and brought to Thranduil in Mirkwood. Gandalf visits Minas Tirith and reads the scroll of Isildur.

THE GREAT YEARS
3018

April

12 Gandalf reaches Hobbiton.

June

20 Sauron attacks Osgiliath. About the same time Thranduil is attacked, and Gollum escapes.

July

4 Boromir sets out from Minas Tirith.
10 Gandalf imprisoned in Orthanc.

August

All trace of Gollum is lost. It is thought that at about this time, being hunted both by the Elves and Sauron's servants, he took refuge in Moria; but when he had at last discovered the way to the West-gate he could not get out.

September

18 Gandalf escapes from Orthanc in the early hours. The Black Riders cross the Fords of Isen.

19 Gandalf comes to Edoras as a beggar, and is refused admittance.

20 Gandalf gains entrance to Edoras. Théoden commands him to go: 'Take any horse, only be gone ere tomorrow is old!'

21 Gandalf meets Shadowfax, but the horse will not allow him to come near. He follows Shadowfax far over the fields.

22 The Black Riders reach Sarn Ford at evening; they drive off the guard of Rangers. Gandalf overtakes Shadowfax.

23 Four Riders enter the Shire before dawn. The others pursue the Rangers eastward, and then return to watch the Greenway. A Black Rider comes to Hobbiton at nightfall. Frodo leaves Bag End. Gandalf having tamed Shadowfax rides from Rohan.

24 Gandalf crosses the Isen.

26 The Old Forest. Frodo comes to Bombadil.

27 Gandalf crosses Greyflood. Second night with Bombadil.

28 The Hobbits captured by a Barrow-wight. Gandalf reaches Sarn Ford.

29 Frodo reaches Bree at night. Gandalf visits the Gaffer.

30 Crickhollow and the Inn at Bree are raided in the early hours. Frodo leaves Bree. Gandalf comes to Crickhollow, and reaches Bree at night.

October

1 Gandalf leaves Bree.

3 He is attacked at night on Weathertop.

6 The camp under Weathertop attacked at night. Frodo wounded.

9 Glorfindel leaves Rivendell.

11 He drives the Riders off the Bridge of Mitheithel.

13 Frodo crosses the Bridge.

18 Glorfindel finds Frodo at dusk. Gandalf reaches Rivendell.

20 Escape across the Ford of Bruinen.

24 Frodo recovers and wakes. Boromir arrives in Rivendell at night.

25 Council of Elrond.

December

25 The Company of the Ring leaves Rivendell at dusk.

3019

January

8   The Company reach Hollin.

11, 12   Snow on Caradhras.

13   Attack by Wolves in the early hours. The Company reaches West-gate of Moria at nightfall. Gollum begins to trail the Ring-bearer.

14   Night in Hall Twenty-one.

15   The Bridge of Khazad-dûm, and fall of Gandalf. The Company reaches Nimrodel late at night.

17   The Company comes to Caras Galadhon at evening.

23   Gandalf pursues the Balrog to the peak of Zirakzigil.

25   He casts down the Balrog, and passes away. His body lies on the peak.

February

14 The Mirror of Galadriel. Gandalf returns to life, and lies in a trance.

16 Farewell to Lórien. Gollum in hiding on the west bank observes the departure.

17 Gwaihir bears Gandalf to Lórien.

23 The boats are attacked at night near Sarn Gebir.

25 The Company pass the Argonath and camp at Parth Galen. First Battle of the Fords of Isen; Théodred son of Théoden slain.

26 Breaking of the Fellowship. Death of Boromir; his horn is heard in Minas Tirith. Meriadoc and Peregrin captured. Frodo and Samwise enter the eastern Emyn Muil. Aragorn sets out in pursuit of the Orcs at evening. Éomer hears of the descent of the Orc-band from Emyn Muil.

27 Aragorn reaches the west-cliff at sunrise. Éomer against Théoden's orders sets out from Eastfold about midnight to pursue the Orcs.

28 Éomer overtakes the Orcs just outside Fangorn Forest.

29 Meriadoc and Pippin escape and meet Treebeard. The Rohirrim attack at sunrise and destroy the Orcs. Frodo descends from the Emyn Muil and meets Gollum. Faramir sees the funeral boat of Boromir.

30 Entmoot begins. Éomer returning to Edoras meets Aragorn.

March

1 Frodo begins the passage of the Dead Marshes at dawn. Entmoot continues. Aragorn meets Gandalf the White. They set out for Edoras. Faramir leaves Minas Tirith on an errand to Ithilien.

2 Frodo comes to the end of the Marshes. Gandalf comes to Edoras and heals Théoden. The Rohirrim ride west against Saruman. Second Battle of Fords of Isen. Erkenbrand defeated. Entmoot ends in afternoon. The Ents march on Isengard and reach it at night.

3 Théoden retreats to Helm's Deep. Battle of the Hornburg begins. Ents complete the destruction of Isengard.

4 Théoden and Gandalf set out from Helm's Deep for Isengard. Frodo reaches the slag-mounds on the edge of the Desolation of the Morannon.

5 Théoden reaches Isengard at noon. Parley with Saruman in Orthanc. Winged Nazgûl passes over the camp at Dol Baran. Gandalf sets out with Peregrin for Minas Tirith. Frodo hides in sight of the Morannon, and leaves at dusk.

6 Aragorn overtaken by the Dúnedain in the early hours. Théoden sets out from the Hornburg for Harrowdale. Aragorn sets out later.

7 Frodo taken by Faramir to Henneth Annûn. Aragorn comes to Dunharrow at nightfall.

8 Aragorn takes the 'Paths of the Dead' at daybreak; he reaches Erech at midnight. Frodo leaves Henneth Annûn.

9 Gandalf reaches Minas Tirith. Faramir leaves Henneth Annûn. Aragorn sets out from Erech and comes to Calembel. At dusk Frodo reaches the Morgul-road. Théoden comes to Dunharrow. Darkness begins to flow out of Mordor.

10 The Dawnless Day. The Muster of Rohan: the Rohirrim ride from Harrowdale. Faramir rescued by Gandalf outside the gates of the City. Aragorn crosses Ringló. An army from the Morannon takes Cair Andros and passes into Anórien. Frodo passes the Cross Roads, and sees the Morgul-host set forth.

11 Gollum visits Shelob, but seeing Frodo asleep nearly repents. Denethor sends Faramir to Osgiliath. Aragorn reaches Linhir and crosses into Lebennin. Eastern Rohan is invaded from the north. First assault on Lórien.

12 Gollum leads Frodo into Shelob's lair. Faramir retreats to the Causeway Forts. Théoden camps under Minrimmon. Aragorn drives the enemy towards Pelargir. The Ents defeat the invaders of Rohan.

13 Frodo captured by the Orcs of Cirith Ungol. The Pelennor is overrun. Faramir is wounded. Aragorn reaches Pelargir and captures the fleet. Théoden in Drúadan Forest.

14 Samwise finds Frodo in the Tower. Minas Tirith is besieged. The Rohirrim led by the Wild Men come to the Grey Wood.

15 In the early hours the Witch-king breaks the Gates of the City. Denethor burns himself on a pyre. The horns of the Rohirrim are heard at cockcrow. Battle of the Pelennor. Théoden is slain. Aragorn raises the standard of Arwen. Frodo and Samwise escape and begin their journey north along the Morgai. Battle under the trees in Mirkwood; Thranduil repels the forces of Dol Guldur. Second assault on Lórien.

16 Debate of the commanders. Frodo from the Morgai looks out over the camp to Mount Doom.

17 Battle of Dale. King Brand and King Dáin Ironfoot fall. Many Dwarves and Men take refuge in Erebor and are besieged. Shagrat brings Frodo's cloak, mail-shirt, and sword to Barad-dûr.

18 The Host of the West marches from Minas Tirith. Frodo comes in sight of the Isenmouthe; he is overtaken by Orcs on the road from Durthang to Udûn.

19 The Host comes to Morgul-vale. Frodo and Samwise escape and begin their journey along the road to the Barad-dûr.

22 The dreadful nightfall. Frodo and Samwise leave the road and turn south to Mount Doom. Third assault on Lórien.

23 The Host passes out of Ithilien. Aragorn dismisses the faint-hearted. Frodo and Samwise cast away their arms and gear.

24 Frodo and Samwise make their last journey to the feet of Mount Doom. The Host camps in the Desolation of the Morannon.

25 The Host is surrounded on the Slag-hills. Frodo and Samwise reach the Sammath Naur. Gollum seizes the Ring and falls in the Cracks of Doom. Downfall of Barad-dûr and passing of Sauron.

After the fall of the Dark Tower and the passing of Sauron the Shadow was lifted from the hearts of all who opposed him, but fear and despair fell upon his servants and allies. Three times Lórien had been assailed from Dol Guldur, but besides the valour of the elven people of that land, the power that dwelt there was too great for any to overcome, unless Sauron had come there himself. Though grievous harm was done to the fair woods on the borders, the assaults were driven back; and when the Shadow passed, Celeborn came forth and led the host of Lórien over Anduin in many boats. They took Dol Guldur, and Galadriel threw down its walls and laid bare its pits, and the forest was cleansed.

In the North also there had been war and evil. The realm of

Thranduil was invaded, and there was long battle under the trees and great ruin of fire; but in the end Thranduil had the victory. And on the day of the New Year of the Elves, Celeborn and Thranduil met in the midst of the forest; and they renamed Mirkwood *Eryn Lasgalen*, The Wood of Greenleaves. Thranduil took all the northern region as far as the mountains that rise in the forest for his realm; and Celeborn took all the southern wood below the Narrows, and named it East Lórien; all the wide forest between was given to the Beornings and the Woodmen. But after the passing of Galadriel in a few years Celeborn grew weary of his realm and went to Imladris to dwell with the sons of Elrond. In the Greenwood the Silvan Elves remained untroubled, but in Lórien there lingered sadly only a few of its former people, and there was no longer light or song in Caras Galadhon.

At the same time as the great armies besieged Minas Tirith a host of the allies of Sauron that had long threatened the borders of King Brand crossed the River Carnen, and Brand was driven back to Dale. There he had the aid of the Dwarves of Erebor; and there was a great battle at the Mountain's feet. It lasted three days, but in the end both King Brand and King Dáin Ironfoot were slain, and the Easterlings had the victory. But they could not take the Gate, and many, both Dwarves and Men, took refuge in Erebor, and there withstood a siege.

When news came of the great victories in the South, then Sauron's northern army was filled with dismay; and the besieged came forth and routed them, and the remnant fled into the East and troubled Dale no more. Then Bard II, Brand's son, became King in Dale, and Thorin III Stonehelm, Dáin's son, became King under the Mountain. They sent their ambassadors to the crowning of King Elessar; and their realms remained ever after, as long as they lasted, in friendship with Gondor; and they were under the crown and protection of the King of the West.

THE CHIEF DAYS
FROM THE FALL OF BARAD-DÛR TO THE END OF THE THIRD AGE[1]

3019
S.R. 1419

March 27. Bard II and Thorin III Stonehelm drive the enemy from Dale.

28. Celeborn crosses Anduin; destruction of Dol Guldur begun.

April 6. Meeting of Celeborn and Thranduil.

8. The Ring-bearers are honoured on the Field of Cormallen.

May 1. Crowning of King Elessar; Elrond and Arwen set out from Rivendell.

8. Éomer and Éowyn depart from Rohan with the sons of Elrond.

20. Elrond and Arwen come to Lórien.

27. The escort of Arwen leaves Lórien.

June 14. The sons of Elrond meet the escort and bring Arwen to Edoras.

16. They set out for Gondor.

25. King Elessar finds the sapling of the White Tree.

1 Lithe. Arwen comes to the City.

Mid-year's Day. Wedding of Elessar and Arwen.

July 18. Éomer returns to Minas Tirith.

19. The funeral escort of King Théoden sets out.

August 7. The escort comes to Edoras.

10. Funeral of King Théoden.

14. The guests take leave of King Éomer.

18. They come to Helm's Deep.

22. They come to Isengard; they take leave of the King of the West at sunset.

28. They overtake Saruman; Saruman turns towards the Shire.

September 6. They halt in sight of the Mountains of Moria.

---

[1] Months and days are given according to the Shire Calendar.

13. Celeborn and Galadriel depart, the others set out for Rivendell.

21. They return to Rivendell.

22. The hundred and twenty-ninth birthday of Bilbo. Saruman comes to the Shire.

October 5. Gandalf and the Hobbits leave Rivendell.

6. They cross the Ford of Bruinen; Frodo feels the first return of pain.

28. They reach Bree at nightfall.

30. They leave Bree. The 'Travellers' come to the Brandywine Bridge at dark.

November 1. They are arrested at Frogmorton.

2. They come to Bywater and rouse the Shire-folk.

3. Battle of Bywater, and Passing of Saruman. End of the War of the Ring.

3020
S.R. 1420: The Great Year of Plenty

March 13. Frodo is taken ill (on the anniversary of his poisoning by Shelob).

April 6. The mallorn flowers in the Party Field.

May 1. Samwise marries Rose.

Mid-year's Day. Frodo resigns office of mayor, and Will Whitfoot is restored.

September 22. Bilbo's hundred and thirtieth birthday.

October 6. Frodo is again ill.

3021
S.R. 1421: The Last of the Third Age

March 13. Frodo is again ill.

25. Birth of Elanor the Fair,[1] daughter of Samwise. On this day the Fourth Age began in the reckoning of Gondor.

[1] She became known as 'the Fair' because of her beauty; many said that she looked more like an elf-maid than a hobbit. She had golden hair, which had been very rare in the Shire; but two others of Samwise's daughters were also golden-haired, and so were many of the children born at this time.

September 21. Frodo and Samwise set out from Hobbiton.

22. They meet the Last Riding of the Keepers of the Rings in Woody End.

29. They come to the Grey Havens. Frodo and Bilbo depart over Sea with the Three Keepers. The end of the Third Age.

October 6. Samwise returns to Bag End.

LATER EVENTS CONCERNING
THE MEMBERS OF THE FELLOWSHIP
OF THE RING

S.R.

1422   With the beginning of this year the Fourth Age began in the count of years in the Shire; but the numbers of the years of Shire Reckoning were continued.

1427   Will Whitfoot resigns. Samwise is elected Mayor of the Shire. Peregrin Took marries Diamond of Long Cleeve. King Elessar issues an edict that Men are not to enter the Shire, and he makes it a Free Land under the protection of the Northern Sceptre.

1430   Faramir, son of Peregrin, born.

1431   Goldilocks, daughter of Samwise, born.

1432   Meriadoc, called the Magnificent, becomes Master of Buckland. Great gifts are sent to him by King Éomer and the Lady Éowyn of Ithilien.

1434   Peregrin becomes the Took and Thain. King Elessar makes the Thain, the Master, and the Mayor Counsellors of the North-kingdom. Master Samwise is elected Mayor for the second time.

1436   King Elessar rides north, and dwells for a while by Lake Evendim. He comes to the Brandywine Bridge, and there greets his friends. He gives the Star of the Dúnedain to Master Samwise, and Elanor is made a maid of honour to Queen Arwen.

1441   Master Samwise becomes Mayor for the third time.

1442   Master Samwise and his wife and Elanor ride to

Gondor and stay there for a year. Master Tolman
Cotton acts as deputy Mayor.

1448   Master Samwise becomes Mayor for the fourth time.

1451   Elanor the Fair marries Fastred of Greenholm on the
Far Downs.

1452   The Westmarch, from the Far Downs to the Tower
Hills (*Emyn Beraid*),[1] is added to the Shire by the
gift of the King. Many hobbits remove to it.

1454   Elfstan Fairbairn, son of Fastred and Elanor, is born.

1455   Master Samwise becomes Mayor for the fifth time.
At his request the Thain makes Fastred Warden of
Westmarch. Fastred and Elanor make their dwelling
at Undertowers on the Tower Hills, where their
descendants, the Fairbairns of the Towers, dwelt for
many generations.

1462   Master Samwise becomes Mayor for the sixth time.

1463   Faramir Took marries Goldilocks, daughter of
Samwise.

1469   Master Samwise becomes Mayor for the seventh and
last time, being in 1476, at the end of his office,
ninety-six years old.

1482   Death of Mistress Rose, wife of Master Samwise, on
Mid-year's Day. On September 22 Master Samwise
rides out from Bag End. He comes to the Tower
Hills, and is last seen by Elanor, to whom he gives
the Red Book afterwards kept by the Fairbairns.
Among them the tradition is handed down from
Elanor that Samwise passed the Towers, and went to
the Grey Havens, and passed over Sea, last of the
Ring-bearers.

1484   In the spring of the year a message came from Rohan
to Buckland that King Éomer wished to see Master
Holdwine once again. Meriadoc was then old (102)
but still hale. He took counsel with his friend the
Thain, and soon after they handed over their goods
and offices to their sons and rode away over the Sarn
Ford, and they were not seen again in the Shire. It

[1] I, p. 12; VII, p. 18, note 2.

was heard after that Master Meriadoc came to Edoras and was with King Éomer before he died in that autumn. Then he and Thain Peregrin went to Gondor and passed what short years were left to them in that realm, until they died and were laid in Rath Dínen among the great of Gondor.

1541   In this year[1] on March 1st came at last the Passing of King Elessar. It is said that the beds of Meriadoc and Peregrin were set beside the bed of the great king. Then Legolas built a grey ship in Ithilien, and sailed down Anduin and so over Sea; and with him, it is said, went Gimli the Dwarf. And when that ship passed an end was come in Middle-earth of the Fellowship of the Ring.

[1] Fourth Age (Gondor) 120.

APPENDIX C

FAMILY TREES

The names given in these Trees are only a selection from many. Most of them are either guests at Bilbo's Farewell Party, or their direct ancestors. The guests at the Party are underlined. A few other names of persons concerned in the events recounted are also given. In addition some genealogical information is provided concerning Samwise the founder of the family of *Gardner*, later famous and influential.

The figures after the names are those of birth (and death where that is recorded). All dates are given according to the Shire-reckoning, calculated from the crossing of the Brandywine by the brothers Marcho and Blanco in the Year 1 of the Shire (Third Age 1601).

BAGGINS OF HOBBITON

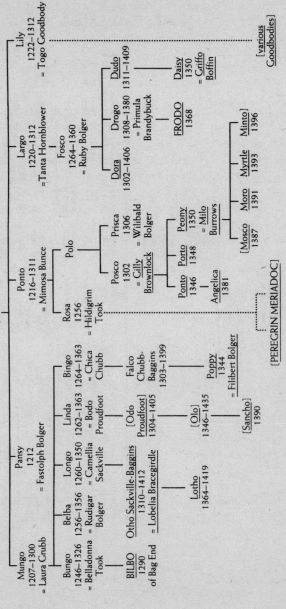

TOOK OF GREAT SMIALS

*Isengrim II
(Tenth Thain of the
Took line)
1020–1122
|
*Isumbras III
1066–1159

Bandobras
(Bullroarer)
1104–1206
|
Many descendants,
including
the North-tooks
of Long Cleeve

*Ferumbras II
1101–1201
|
*Fortinbras I
1145–1248

*Gerontius, The Old Took
1190–1320
= Adamanta Chubb

Hildifons
1244
(went off on
a journey
and never
returned)

Isembard
1247–1346
|
Flambard
1287–1389

Hildibrand
1249–1334
|
Sigismond
1290–1391

Belladonna
1252–1334
= Bungo
Baggins
|
[BILBO]

Donnamira
1256–1348
= Hugo
Boffin

Mirabella
1260–1360
= Gorbadoc
Brandybuck
q.v.

Isengar
1262–1360
(said to have
gone to
sea' in
his youth)

[Primula]
|
[FRODO]

[six
children]

Adelard
1328–1423

Rosamunda
1338
= Odovacar
Bolger

Ferdinand
1340
|
Ferdibrand
1383

Reginard
1369

3 daughters

[Fredegar]
1380

[Estella]
1385

Everard
1380

Isembold
1242–1346
|
(many
descendants)

Esmeralda
1336
= Saradoc
Brandybuck
|
[MERIADOC]

Isumbras IV
1238–1339

Hildigrim
1240–1341
= Rosa Baggins
|
Adalgrim
1280–1382

*Paladin II
1333–1434
= Eglantine Banks

3 daughters

*PEREGRIN I
1390
= Diamond of
Long Cleeve
1395
|
*Faramir I
1430

Pervinca
1385

Isengrim III
1232–1330
(no children)

Hildigard
(died young)

*Fortinbras II
1278–1380

*Ferumbras III
1316–1415
(unmarried)

Pimpernel
1379

Pearl
1375

= Goldilocks daughter of Master Samwise

BRANDYBUCK OF BUCKLAND

Gorhendad Oldbuck of the Marish, c. 740 began the building of *Brandy Hall* and changed the family name to *Brandybuck*.

Gormadoc 'Deepdelver'
1134–1236
= Malva Headstrong

Marroc
(many descendants)

Sadoc 1179

Two Sons
(various descendants)

Salvia 1226
= Gundabald Bolger

Madoc 'Proudneck'
1175–1277
= Hanna Goldworthy

Marmadoc 'Masterful'
1217–1310
= Adaldrida Bolger

Orgulas 1268

Gorbulas 1308

Marmadas 1343

Merimas 1381

Mentha 1383

Melilot 1385

Gorbadoc 'Broadbelt'
1260–1363
= Mirabella Took

(Two daughters)

Primula 1320–1380
= Drogo Baggins

[FRODO] Baggins

Dinodas

Asphodel 1313–1412
= Rufus Burrows

[Milo Burrows] 1347
= Peony Baggins

Dodinas

Saradas 1308–1407

Seredic 1348
= Hilda Bracegirdle

Doderic 1389

Ilberic 1391

Celandine 1394

Amaranth 1304–1398

Rorimac 'Goldfather'
(Old Rory) 1302–1408
= Menegilda Goold

Merimac 1342–1430

Berilac 1380

Saradoc 'Scattergold'
1340–1432
= Esmeralda Took

MERIADOC
'the Magnificent' 1382
= Estella Bolger 1385

THE LONGFATHER-TREE OF MASTER SAMWISE

(showing also the rise of the families of Gardner of the Hill and of Fairbairn of the Towers.)

Hamfast of Gamwich 1160

Wiseman Gamwich 1200 (removed to Tighfield)

Holman, the greenhanded, of Hobbiton 1210

Cottar 1220

Hob Gammidge the Roper ('Old Gammidgy') 1246 = Rowan 1249

Halfred Greenhand 1251 (gardener)

Erling 1254

Hending 1259

Rose 1262 = Cotman 1260

Carl 1263

Hobson (Roper Gamgee) 1285–1384

Holman Greenhand 1292

Holman Cotton ('Long Hom') of Bywater 1302

HAMFAST (Ham Gamgee) the Gaffer 1326–1428 = Bell Goodchild

took up with his 'Cousin Holman' in Hobbiton as a gardener

May 1328

Halfred of Overhill 1332

Tolman Cotton ('Tom') 1341–1440 = Lily Brown

Wilcome ('Will') 1346

Andwise Roper of Tighfield ('Andy') 1323

Hamson 1365 (joined his uncle, the roper)

Halfred 1369

Daisy 1372

May 1376

SAMWISE 1380 (gardener) = Rose Cotton

Margold = Tolman 1383   (Tom) 1380

Halfast 1372

ROSE 1384 = Sam Gamgee

Wilcome (Jolly) 1384

Bowman (Nick) 1386

Carl (Nibs) 1389

Anson 1361

ELANOR the Fair 1421 = Fastred of Greenholm

FRODO Gardner 1423

Rose Gardner 1425

Merry 1427

Pippin 1429

GOLDILOCKS 1431 = Faramir I son of Thain Peregrin I

Hamfast 1432

Daisy 1433

Primrose 1435

Bilbo 1436

Ruby 1438

Robin 1440

Tolman (Tom) 1442

Holfast Gardner 1462

Harding of the Hill 1501

They removed to the *Westmarch*, a country then newly settled (being a gift of King Elessar) between the Far Downs and the Tower Hills. From them came the *Fairbairns of the Towers*, Wardens of Westmarch, who inherited the Red Book, and made several copies with various notes and later additions.

APPENDIX D

SHIRE CALENDAR

FOR USE IN ALL YEARS

(1) *Afteryule*	(4) *Astron*	(7) *Afterlithe*	(10) *Winterfilth*
YULE 7 14 21 28	1　8 15 22 29	LITHE 7 14 21 28	1　8 15 22 29
1　8 15 22 29	2　9 16 23 30	1　8 15 22 29	2　9 16 23 30
2　9 16 23 30	3 10 17 24 −	2　9 16 23 30	3 10 17 24 −
3 10 17 24 −	4 11 18 25 −	3 10 17 24 −	4 11 18 25 −
4 11 18 25 −	5 12 19 26 −	4 11 18 25 −	5 12 19 26 −
5 12 19 26 −	6 13 20 27 −	5 12 19 26 −	6 13 20 27 −
6 13 20 27 −	7 14 21 28 −	6 13 20 27 −	7 14 21 28 −

(2) *Solmath*	(5) *Thrimidge*	(8) *Wedmath*	(11) *Blotmath*
− 5 12 19 26	− 6 13 20 27	− 5 12 19 26	− 6 13 20 27
− 6 13 20 27	− 7 14 21 28	− 6 13 20 27	− 7 14 21 28
− 7 14 21 28	1　8 15 22 29	− 7 14 21 28	1　8 15 22 29
1　8 15 22 29	2　9 16 23 30	1　8 15 22 29	2　9 16 23 30
2　9 16 23 30	3 10 17 24 −	2　9 16 23 30	3 10 17 24 −
3 10 17 24 −	4 11 18 25 −	3 10 17 24 −	4 11 18 25 −
4 11 18 25 −	5 12 19 26 −	4 11 18 25 −	5 12 19 26 −

(3) *Rethe*	(6) *Forelithe*	(9) *Halimath*	(12) *Foreyule*
− 3 10 17 24	− 4 11 18 25	− 3 10 17 24	− 4 11 18 25
− 4 11 18 25	− 5 12 19 26	− 4 11 18 25	− 5 12 19 26
− 5 12 19 26	− 6 13 20 27	− 5 12 19 26	− 6 13 20 27
− 6 13 20 27	− 7 14 21 28	− 6 13 20 27	− 7 14 21 28
− 7 14 21 28	1　8 15 22 29	− 7 14 21 28	1　8 15 22 29
1　8 15 22 29	2　9 16 23 30	1　8 15 22 29	2　9 16 23 30
2　9 16 23 30	3 10 17 24 LITHE	2　9 16 23 30	3 10 17 24 YULE
	Midyear's Day		
	(Overlithe)		

Every year began on the first day of the week, Saturday, and
ended on the last day of the week, Friday. The Mid-year's Day,
and in Leap-years the Overlithe, had no weekday name. The

Lithe before Mid-year's Day was called 1 Lithe, and the one after was called 2 Lithe. The Yule at the end of the year was 1 Yule, and that at the beginning was 2 Yule. The Overlithe was a day of special holiday, but it did not occur in any of the years important to the history of the Great Ring. It occurred in 1420, the year of the famous harvest and wonderful summer, and the merrymaking in that year is said to have been the greatest in memory or record.

THE CALENDARS

The Calendar in the Shire differed in several features from ours. The year no doubt was of the same length,[1] for long ago as those times are now reckoned in years and lives of men, they were not very remote according to the memory of the Earth. It is recorded by the Hobbits that they had no 'week' when they were still a wandering people, and though they had 'months', governed more or less by the Moon, their keeping of dates and calculations of time were vague and inaccurate. In the west-lands of Eriador, when they had begun to settle down, they adopted the King's reckoning of the Dúnedain, which was ultimately of Eldarin origin; but the Hobbits of the Shire introduced several minor alterations. This calendar, or 'Shire Reckoning' as it was called, was eventually adopted also in Bree, except for the Shire usage of counting as Year 1 the year of the colonization of the Shire.

It is often difficult to discover from old tales and traditions precise information about things which people knew well and took for granted in their own day (such as the names of letters, or of the days of the week, or the names and lengths of months). But owing to their general interest in genealogy, and to the interest in ancient history which the learned amongst them developed after the War of the Ring, the Shire-hobbits seem to have concerned themselves a good deal with dates; and they even drew up complicated tables showing the relations of their own system with others. I am not skilled in these matters, and may have made many errors; but at any rate the chronology of

---

[1] 365 days, 5 hours, 48 minutes, 46 seconds.

the crucial years S.R. 1418, 1419 is so carefully set out in the Red Book that there cannot be much doubt about days and times at that point.

It seems clear that the Eldar in Middle-earth, who had, as Samwise remarked, more time at their disposal, reckoned in long periods, and the Quenya word *yén*, often translated 'year' (I, p. 496), really means 144 of our years. The Eldar preferred to reckon in sixes and twelves as far as possible. A 'day' of the sun they called *ré* and reckoned from sunset to sunset. The *yén* contained 52,596 days. For ritual rather than practical purposes the Eldar observed a week or *enquië* of six days; and the *yén* contained 8,766 of these *enquier*, reckoned continuously throughout the period.

In Middle-earth the Eldar also observed a short period or solar year, called a *coranar* or 'sun-round' when considered more or less astronomically, but usually called *loa* 'growth' (especially in the north-western lands) when the seasonal changes in vegetation were primarily considered, as was usual with the Elves generally. The *loa* was broken up into periods that might be regarded either as long months or short seasons. These no doubt varied in different regions; but the Hobbits only provide information concerning the Calendar of Imladris. In that calendar there were six of these 'seasons', of which the Quenya names were *tuilë, lairë, yávië, quellë, hrívë, coirë*, which may be translated 'spring, summer, autumn, fading, winter, stirring'. The Sindarin names were *ethuil, laer, iavas, firith, rhîw, echuir*. 'Fading' was also called *lasse-lanta* 'leaf-fall', or in Sindarin *narbeleth* 'sun-waning'.

Lairë and *hrívë* each contained 72 days, and the remainder 54 each. The *loa* began with *yestarë*, the day immediately before *tuilë*, and ended with *mettarë*, the day immediately after *coirë*. Between *yávië* and *quellë* were inserted three *enderi* or 'middle-days'. This provided a year of 365 days which was supplemented by doubling the *enderi* (adding 3 days) in every twelfth year.

How any resulting inaccuracy was dealt with is uncertain. If the year was then of the same length as now, the *yén* would have been more than a day too long. That there was an inaccuracy is shown by a note in the Calendars of the Red Book to the effect that in the 'Reckoning of Rivendell' the last year of every third *yén* was shortened by three days: the doubling of the three *enderi* due in that year was omitted; 'but that has not happened in our time'. Of the adjustment of any remaining inaccuracy there is no record.

The Númenoreans altered these arrangements. They divided the *loa* into shorter periods of more regular length; and they adhered to the custom of beginning the year in mid-winter, which had been used by Men of the North-west from whom they were derived in the First Age. Later they also made their week one of 7 days, and they reckoned the day from sunrise (out of the eastern sea) to sunrise.

The Númenorean system, as used in Númenor, and in Arnor and Gondor until the end of the kings, was called King's Reckoning. The normal year had 365 days. It was divided into twelve *astar* or months, of which ten had 30 days and two had 31. The long *astar* were those on either side of the Mid-year, approximately our June and July. The first day of the year was called *yestarë*, the middle day (183rd) was called *loëndë*, and the last day *mettarë*; these 3 days belonged to no month. In every fourth year, except the last of a century (*haranyë*), two *enderi* or 'middle-days' were substituted for the *loëndë*.

In Númenor calculation started with S.A. 1. The *Deficit* caused by deducting 1 day from the last year of a century was not adjusted until the last year of a millennium, leaving a *millennial deficit* of 4 hours, 46 minutes, 40 seconds. This addition was made in Númenor in S.A. 1000, 2000, 3000. After the Downfall in S.A. 3319 the system was maintained by the exiles, but it was much dislocated by the beginning of the Third Age with a new numeration: S.A. 3442 became T.A. 1. By making T.A. 4 a leap year instead of T.A. 3 (S.A. 3444) 1 more short year of only 365 days was intruded causing a deficit of 5 hours, 48 minutes, 46 seconds. The millennial additions were made 441 years late: in T.A. 1000 (S.A. 4441) and 2000 (S.A. 5441). To reduce the errors so caused, and the accumulation of the millennial deficits, Mardil the Steward issued a revised calendar to take effect in T.A. 2060, after a special addition of 2 days to 2059 (S.A. 5500), which concluded 5½ millennia since the beginning of the Númenorean system. But this still left about 8 hours deficit.

Hador to 2360 added 1 day though this deficiency had not quite reached that amount. After that no more adjustments were made. (In T.A. 3000 with the threat of imminent war such matters were neglected.) By the end of the Third Age, after 660 more years, the Deficit had not yet amounted to 1 day.

The Revised Calendar introduced by Mardil was called Stewards' Reckoning and was adopted eventually by most of the users of the Westron language, except the Hobbits. The months were all of 30 days, and 2 days outside the months were introduced: 1 between the third and four months (March, April), and 1 between the ninth and tenth (September, October). These 5 days outside the months, *yestarë*, *tuilérë*, *loëndë*, *yáviérë*, and *mettarë*, were holidays.

The Hobbits were conservative and continued to use a form of Kings' Reckoning adapted to fit their own customs. Their months were all equal and had 30 days each; but they had 3 Summerdays, called in the Shire the Lithe or the Lithedays, between June and July. The last day of the year and the first of the next year were called the Yuledays. The Yuledays and the Lithedays remained outside the months, so that January 1 was the second and not the first day of the year. Every fourth year, except in the last year of the century,[1] there were four Lithedays. The Lithedays and the Yuledays were the chief holidays and times of feasting. The additional Litheday was added after Mid-year's Day, and so the 184th day of the Leap-years was called Overlithe and was a day of special merrymaking. In full Yuletide was six days long, including the last three and first three days of each year.

The Shire-folk introduced one small innovation of their own (eventually also adopted in Bree), which they called Shire-reform. They found the shifting of the weekday names in relation to dates from year to year untidy and inconvenient. So in the time of Isengrim II they arranged that the odd day which put the succession out, should have no weekday name. After that Mid-year's Day (and the Overlithe) was known only by its name

---

[1] In the Shire, in which Year 1 corresponded with T.A. 1601. In Bree in which Year 1 corresponded with T.A. 1300 it was the first year of the century.

and belonged to no week (I, p. 224). In consequence of this reform the year always began on the First Day of the week and ended on the Last Day; and the same date in any one year had the same weekday name in all other years, so that Shire-folk no longer bothered to put the weekday in their letters or diaries.[1] They found this quite convenient at home, but not so convenient if they ever travelled further than Bree.

In the above notes, as in the narrative, I have used our modern names for both months and weekdays, though of course neither the Eldar nor the Dúnedain nor the Hobbits actually did so. Translation of the Westron names seemed to be essential to avoid confusion, while the seasonal implications of our names are more or less the same, at any rate in the Shire. It appears, however, that Mid-year's Day was intended to correspond as nearly as possible to the summer solstice. In that case the Shire dates were actually in advance of ours by some ten days, and our New Year's Day corresponded more or less to the Shire January 9.

In the Westron the Quenya names of the months were usually retained as the Latin names are now widely used in alien languages. They were: *Narvinyë, Nénimë, Súlimë, Víressë, Lótessë, Nárië, Cermië, Urimë, Yavannië, Narquelië, Hísimë, Ringarë*. The Sindarin names (used only by the Dúnedain) were: *Narwain, Nínui, Gwaeron, Gwirith, Lothron, Nórui, Cerveth, Urui, Ivanneth, Narbeleth, Hithui, Girithron.*

In this nomenclature the Hobbits, however, both of the Shire and of Bree, diverged from the Westron usage, and adhered to old-fashioned local names of their own, which they seem to have picked up in antiquity from the Men of the vales of Anduin; at any rate similar names were found in Dale and Rohan (cf. the notes on the languages, pp. 134–5).

---

[1] It will be noted if one glances at a Shire Calendar, that the only weekday on which no month began was Friday. It thus became a jesting idiom in the Shire to speak of 'on Friday the first' when referring to a day that did not exist, or to a day on which very unlikely events such as the flying of pigs or (in the Shire) the walking of trees might occur. In full the expression was 'on Friday the first of Summerfilth'.

The meanings of these names, devised by Men, had as a rule long been forgotten by the Hobbits, even in cases where they had originally known what their significance was; and the forms of the names were much obscured in consequence: *math*, for instance, at the end of some of them is a reduction of *month*.

The Shire names are set out in the Calendar. It may be noted that *Solmath* was usually pronounced, and sometimes written, *Somath*; *Thrimidge* was often written *Thrimich* (archaically *Thrimilch*); and *Blotmath* was pronounced *Blodmath* or *Blommath*. In Bree the names differed, being *Frery, Solmath, Rethe, Chithing, Thrimidge, Lithe, The Summerdays, Mede, Wedmath, Harvestmath, Wintring, Blooting*, and *Yulemath. Frery, Chithing* and *Yulemath* were also used in the Eastfarthing.[1]

The Hobbit week was taken from the Dúnedain, and the names were translations of those given to the days in the old North-kingdom, which in their turn were derived from the Eldar. The six-day week of the Eldar had days dedicated to, or named after, the Stars, the Sun, the Moon, the Two Trees, the Heavens, and the Valar or Powers, in that order, the last day being the chief day of the week. Their names in Quenya were *Elenya, Anarya, Isilya, Aldúya, Menelya, Valanya* (or *Tárion*); the Sindarin names were *Orgilion, Oranor, Orithil, Orgaladhad, Ormenel, Orbelain* (or *Rodyn*).

The Númenoreans retained the dedications and order, but altered the fourth day to *Aldëa* (*Orgaladh*) with reference to the White Tree only, of which Nimloth that grew in the King's Court in Númenor was believed to be a descendant. Also desiring a seventh day, and being great mariners, they inserted a 'Sea-day', *Eärenya* (*Oraearon*), after the Heavens' Day.

The Hobbits took over this arrangement, but the meanings of their translated names were soon forgotten, or no longer attended to, and the forms were much reduced, especially in everyday

[1] It was a jest in Bree to speak of 'Winterfilth in the (muddy) Shire', but according to the Shire-folk Wintring was a Bree alteration of the older name, which had originally referred to the filling or completion of the year before Winter, and descended from times before the full adoption of Kings' Reckoning when their new year began after harvest.

pronunciation. The first translation of the Númenorean names was probably made two thousand years or more before the end of the Third Age, when the week of the Dúnedain (the feature of their reckoning earliest adopted by alien peoples) was taken up by Men in the North. As with their names of months, the Hobbits adhered to these translations, although elsewhere in the Westron area the Quenya names were used.

Not many ancient documents were preserved in the Shire. At the end of the Third Age far the most notable survival was Yellowskin, or the Yearbook of Tuckborough.[1] Its earliest entries seem to have begun at least nine hundred years before Frodo's time; and many are cited in the Red Book annals and genealogies. In these the weekday names appear in archaic forms, of which the following are the oldest: (1) *Sterrendei*, (2) *Sunnendei*, (3) *Monendei*, (4) *Trewesdei*, (5) *Hevenesdei*, (6) *Meresdei*, (7) *Highdei*. In the language of the time of the War of the Ring these had become *Sterday, Sunday, Monday, Trewsday, Hevensday* (or *Hensday*), *Mersday, Highday*.

I have translated these names also into our own names, naturally beginning with Sunday and Monday, which occur in the Shire week with the same names as ours, and re-naming the others in order. It must be noted, however, that the associations of the names were quite different in the Shire. The last day of the week, Friday (Highday), was the chief day, and one of holiday (after noon) and evening feasts. Saturday thus corresponds more nearly to our Monday, and Thursday to our Saturday.[2]

A few other names may be mentioned that have a reference to time, though not used in precise reckonings. The seasons usually named were *tuilë* spring, *lairë* summer, *yávië* autumn (or harvest), *hrivë* winter; but these had no exact definitions, and *quellë* (or *lasselanta*) was also used for the latter part of autumn and the beginning of winter.

The Eldar paid special attention to the 'twilight' (in the north-

---

[1] Recording births, marriages, and deaths in the Took families, as well as matters, such as land-sales, and various Shire events.

[2] I have therefore in Bilbo's song (I, pp. 209–11) used Saturday and Sunday instead of Thursday and Friday.

erly regions), chiefly as the times of star-fading and star-opening. They had many names for these periods, of which the most usual were *tindómë* and *undómë*; the former most often referred to the time near dawn, and *undómë* to the evening. The Sindarin name was *uial*, which could be defined as *minuial* and *aduial*. These were often called in the Shire *morrowdim* and *evendim*. Cf. Lake Evendim as a translation of Nenuial.

The Shire Reckoning and dates are the only ones of importance for the narrative of the War of the Ring. All the days, months, and dates are in the Red Book translated into Shire terms, or equated with them in notes. The months and days, therefore, throughout *The Lord of the Rings* refer to the Shire Calendar. The only points in which the differences between this and our calendar are important to the story at the crucial period, the end of 3018 and the beginning of 3019 (S.R. 1418, 1419), are these: October 1418 has only 30 days, January 1 is the second day of 1419, and February has 30 days; so that March 25, the date of the downfall of the Barad-dûr, would correspond to our March 27, if our years began at the same seasonal point. The date was, however, March 25 in both Kings' and Stewards' Reckoning.

The New Reckoning was begun in the restored Kingdom in T.A. 3019. It represented a return to Kings' Reckoning adapted to fit a spring-beginning as in the Eldarin *loa*.[1]

In the New Reckoning the year began on March 25 old style, in commemoration of the fall of Sauron and the deeds of the Ring-bearers. The months retained their former names, beginning now with *Viressë* (April), but referred to periods beginning generally five days earlier than previously. All the months had 30 days. There were 3 *Enderi* or Middle-days (of which the second was called *Loëndë*), between *Yavannië* (September) and *Narquelië* (October), that corresponded with September 23, 24, 25 old style. But in honour of Frodo *Yavannië* 30, which corresponded with former September 22, his birthday, was made a

---

[1] Though actually the *yestarë* of New Reckoning occurred earlier than in the Calendar of Imladris, in which it corresponded more or less with Shire April 6.

festival, and the leap-year was provided for by doubling this feast, called *Cormarë* or Ringday.

The Fourth Age was held to have begun with the departure of Master Elrond, which took place in September 3021; but for purposes of record in the Kingdom Fourth Age 1 was the year that began according to the New Reckoning in March 25, 3021, old style.

This reckoning was in the course of the reign of King Elessar adopted in all his lands except the Shire, where the old calendar was retained and Shire Reckoning was continued. Fourth Age 1 was thus called 1422; and in so far as the Hobbits took any account of the change of Age, they maintained that it began with 2 Yule 1422, and not in the previous March.

There is no record of the Shire-folk commemorating either March 25 or September 22; but in the Westfarthing, especially in the country round Hobbiton Hill, there grew up a custom of making holiday and dancing in the Party Field, when weather permitted, on April 6. Some said that it was old Sam Gardner's birthday, some that it was the day on which the Golden Tree first flowered in 1420, and some that it was the Elves' New Year. In the Buckland the Horn of the Mark was blown at sundown every November 2 and bonfires and feastings followed.[1]

---

[1] Anniversary of its first blowing in the Shire in 3019.

APPENDIX E

WRITING AND SPELLING

I
PRONUNCIATION OF WORDS AND NAMES

The Westron or Common Speech has been entirely translated into English equivalents. All Hobbit names and special words are intended to be pronounced accordingly: for example, *Bolger* has *g* as in *bulge*, and *mathom* rhymes with *fathom*.

In transcribing the ancient scripts I have tried to represent the original sounds (so far as they can be determined) with fair accuracy, and at the same time to produce words and names that do not look uncouth in modern letters. The High-elven Quenya has been spelt as much like Latin as its sounds allowed. For this reason *c* has been preferred to *k* in both Eldarin languages.

The following points may be observed by those who are interested in such details.

CONSONANTS

C   has always the value of *k* even before *e* and *i*: *celeb* 'silver' should be pronounced as *keleb*.

CH   is only used to represent the sound heard in *bach* (in German or Welsh), not that in English *church*. Except at the end of words and before *t* this sound was weakened to *h* in the speech of Gondor, and that change has been recognized in a few names, such as *Rohan, Rohirrim*. (*Imrahil* is a Númenorean name.)

DH   represents the voiced (soft) *th* of English *these clothes*. It is usually related to *d*, as in S. *galadh* 'tree' compared with Q. *alda*; but is sometimes derived from *n + r*, as in *Caradhras* 'Redhorn' from *caran-rass*.

F   represents *f*, except at the end of words, where it is used to represent the sound of *v* (as in English *of*): *Nindalf*, *Fladrif*.

G   has only the sound of *g* in *give, get*: *gil* 'star', in *Gildor*, *Gilraen*, *Osgiliath*, begins as in English *gild*.

H   standing alone with no other consonant has the sound of *h* in *house, behold*. The Quenya combination *ht* has the sound of *cht*, as in German *echt, acht*: e.g. in the name *Telumehtar* 'Orion'.[1] See also CH, DH, L, R, TH, W, Y.

I   initially before another vowel has the consonantal sound of *y* in *you, yore* in Sindarin only: as in *Ioreth, Iarwain*. See Y.

K   is used in names drawn from other than Elvish languages, with the same value as *c*; *kh* thus represents the same sound as *ch* in Orkish *Grishnákh*, or Adûnaic (Númenorean) *Adûnakhôr*. On Dwarvish (Khuzdul) see note below.

L   represents more or less the sound of English initial *l*, as in *let*. It was, however, to some degree 'palatalized' between *e*, *i* and a consonant, or finally after *e, i*. (The Eldar would probably have transcribed English *bell, fill* as *beol, fiol*.) LH represents this sound when voiceless (usually derived from initial *sl-*). In (archaic) Quenya this is written *hl*, but was in the Third Age usually pronounced as *l*.

NG   represents *ng* in *finger*, except finally where it was sounded as in English *sing*. The latter sound also occurred initially in Quenya, but has been transcribed *n* (as in *Noldo*), according to the pronunciation of the Third Age.

PH   has the same sound as *f*. It is used *(a)* where the *f*-sound occurs at the end of a word, as in *alph* 'swan'; *(b)* where the *f*-sound is related to or derived from a *p*, as in *i-Pheriannath* 'the Halflings' (*perian*); *(c)* in the middle of a few words where it represents a long *ff* (from *pp*) as in *Ephel* 'outer fence'; and *(d)* in Adûnaic and Westron, as in *Ar-Pharazôn* (*pharaz* 'gold').

QU   has been used for *cw*, a combination very frequent in Quenya, though it did not occur in Sindarin.

R   represents a trilled *r* in all positions; the sound was not

---

[1] Usually called in Sindarin *Menelvagor* (I, p. 108), Q. *Menelmacar*.

lost before consonants (as in English *part*). The Orcs, and some Dwarves, are said to have used a back or uvular *r*, a sound which the Eldar found distasteful. RH represents a voiceless *r* (usually derived from older initial *sr-*). It was written *hr* in Quenya. Cf. L.

S   is always voiceless, as in English *so*, *geese*; the *z*-sound did not occur in contemporary Quenya or Sindarin. SH, occurring in Westron, Dwarvish and Orkish, represents sounds similar to *sh* in English.

TH   represents the voiceless *th* of English in *thin cloth*. This had become *s* in spoken Quenya, though still written with a different letter; as in Q. *Isil*, S. *Ithil*, 'Moon'.

TY   represents a sound probably similar to the *t* in English *tune*. It was derived mainly from *c* or *t + y*. The sound of English *ch*, which was frequent in Westron, was usually substituted for it by speakers of that language. Cf. HY under Y.

V   has the sound of English *v*, but is not used finally. See F.

W   has the sound of English *w*. HW is a voiceless *w*, as in English *white* (in northern pronunciation). It was not an uncommon initial sound in Quenya, though examples seem not to occur in this book. Both *v* and *w* are used in the transcription of Quenya, in spite of the assimilation of its spelling to Latin, since the two sounds, distinct in origin, both occurred in the language.

Y   is used in Quenya for the consonant *y*, as in English *you*. In Sindarin *y* is a vowel (see below). HY has the same relation to *y* as HW to *w*, and represents a sound like that often heard in English *hew*, *huge*; *h* in Quenya *eht*, *iht* had the same sound. The sound of English *sh*, which was common in Westron, was often substituted by speakers of that language. Cf. TY above. HY was usually derived from *sy-* and *khy-*; in both cases related Sindarin words show initial *h*, as in Q. *Hyarmen* 'south', S. *Harad*.

Note that consonants written twice, as *tt*, *ll*, *ss*, *nn*, represent long, 'double' consonants. At the end of words of more than one syllable these were usually shortened: as in *Rohan* from *Rochann* (archaic *Rochand*).

In Sindarin the combinations *ng, nd, mb*, which were specially favoured in the Eldarin languages at an earlier stage, suffered various changes. *mb* became *m* in all cases, but still counted as a long consonant for purposes of stress (see below), and is thus written *mm* in cases where otherwise the stress might be in doubt.[1] *ng* remained unchanged except initially and finally where it became the simple nasal (as in English *sing*). *nd* became *nn* usually, as *Ennor* 'Middle-earth', Q. *Endóre*; but remained *nd* at the end of fully accented monosyllables such as *thond* 'root' (cf. *Morthond* 'Blackroot'), and also before *r*, as *Andros* 'long-foam'. This *nd* is also seen in some ancient names derived from an older period, such as *Nargothrond, Gondolin, Beleriand*. In the Third Age final *nd* in long words had become *n* from *nn*, as in *Ithilien, Rohan, Anórien*.

VOWELS

For vowels the letters *i, e, a, o, u* are used, and (in Sindarin only) *y*. As far as can be determined the sounds represented by these letters (other than *y*) were of normal kind, though doubtless many local varieties escape detection. That is, the sounds were approximately those represented by *i, e, a, o, u* in English *machine, were, father, for, brute*, irrespective of quantity.

In Sindarin long *e, a, o* had the same quality as the short vowels, being derived in comparatively recent times from them (older *é, á, ó* had been changed). In Quenya long *é* and *ó* were, when correctly[2] pronounced, as by the Eldar, tenser and 'closer' than the short vowels.

---

[1] As in *galadhremmin ennorath* (II, p. 29) 'tree-woven lands of Middle-earth'. *Remmirath* (I, p. 108) contains *rem* 'mesh', Q. *rembe*, + *mîr* 'jewel'.

[2] A fairly widespread pronunciation of long *é* and *ó* as *ei* and *ou*, more or less as in English *say no*, both in Westron and in the renderings of Quenya names by Westron speakers, is shown by spellings such as *ei*, *ou* (or their equivalents in contemporary scripts). But such pronunciations were regarded as incorrect or rustic. They were naturally usual in the Shire. Those therefore who pronounce *yéni únótime* 'long-years innumerable', as is natural in English (*sc.* more or less as *yainy oonoatimy*) will err little more than Bilbo, Meriadoc, or Peregrin. Frodo said to have shown great 'skill with foreign sounds'.

Sindarin alone among contemporary languages possessed the 'modified' or fronted *u*, more or less as *u* in French *lune*. It was partly a modification of *o* and *u*, partly derived from older diphthongs *eu*, *iu*. For this sound *y* has been used (as in ancient English): as in *lyg* 'snake', Q. *leuca*, or *emyn* pl. of *amon* 'hill'. In Gondor this *y* was usually pronounced like *i*.

Long vowels are usually marked with the 'acute accent', as in some varieties of Fëanorian script. In Sindarin long vowels in stressed monosyllables are marked with the circumflex, since they tended in such cases to be specially prolonged;[1] so in *dûn* compared with *Dúnadan*. The use of the circumflex in other languages such as Adûnaic or Dwarvish has no special significance, and is used merely to mark these out as alien tongues (as with the use of *k*).

Final *e* is never mute or a mere sign of length as in English. To mark this final *e* it is often (but not consistently) written *ë*.

The groups *er*, *ir*, *ur* (finally or before a consonant) are not intended to be pronounced as in English *fern*, *fir*, *fur*, but rather as English *air*, *eer*, *oor*.

In Quenya *ui*, *oi*, *ai* and *iu*, *eu*, *au* are diphthongs (that is, pronounced in one syllable). All other pairs of vowels are dissyllabic. This is often dictated by writing *ëa* (*Eä*), *ëo*, *oë*.

In Sindarin the diphthongs are written *ae*, *ai*, *ei*, *oe*, *ui*, and *au*. Other combinations are not diphthongal. The writing of final *au* as *aw* is in accordance with English custom, but is actually not uncommon in Fëanorian spellings.

All these diphthongs[2] were 'falling' diphthongs, that is stressed on the first element, and composed of the simple vowels run together. Thus *ai*, *ei*, *oi*, *ui* are intended to be pronounced respectively as the vowels in English *rye* (not *ray*), *grey*, *boy*,

---

[1] So also in *Annûn* 'sunset', *Amrûn* 'sunrise', under the influence of the related *dûn* 'west', and *rhûn* 'east'.

[2] Originally. But *iu* in Quenya was in the Third Age usually pronounced as a rising dipthong as *yu* in English *yule*.

ruin; and *au* (*aw*) as in *loud, how* and not as in *laud, haw.*

There is nothing in English closely corresponding to *ae, oe, eu*; *ae* and *oe* may be pronounced as *ai, oi.*

STRESS

The position of the 'accent' or stress is not marked, since in the Eldarin languages concerned its place is determined by the form of the word. In words of two syllables it falls in practically all cases on the first syllable. In longer words it falls on the last syllable but one, where that contains a long vowel, a diphthong, or a vowel followed by two (or more) consonants. Where the last syllable but one contains (as often) a short vowel followed by only one (or no) consonant, the stress falls on the syllable before it, the third from the end. Words of the last form are favoured in the Eldarin languages, especially Quenya.

In the following examples the stressed vowel is marked by a capital letter: *isIldur, Orome, erEssëa, fËanor, ancAlima, elentÁri, dEnethor, periAnnath, ecthElion, pelArgir, silIvren.* Words of the type *elentÁri* 'star-queen' seldom occur in Quenya where the vowel is *é, á, ó,* unless (as in this case) they are compounds; they are commoner with the vowels *i, ú,* as *andÚne* 'sunset, west'. They do not occur in Sindarin except in compounds. Note that Sindarin *dh, th, ch* are single consonants and represent single letters in the original scripts.

NOTE

In names drawn from other languages than Eldarin the same values for the letters are intended, where not specially described above, except in the case of Dwarvish. In Dwarvish, which did not possess the sounds represented above by *th* and *ch* (*kh*), *th* and *kh* are aspirates, that is *t* or *k* followed by an *h*, more or less as in *backhand, outhouse.*

Where *z* occurs the sound intended is that of English *z. gh* in the Black Speech and Orkish represents a 'back spirant' (related to *g* as *dh* to *d*): as in *ghâsh* and *agh.*

The 'outer' or Mannish names of the Dwarves have been given Northern forms, but the letter-values are those described.

So also in the case of the personal and place-names of Rohan (where they have not been modernized), except that here *éa* and *éo* are diphthongs, which may be represented by the *ea* of English *bear*, and the *eo* of *Theobald*; *y* is the modified *u*. The modernized forms are easily recognized and are intended to be pronounced as in English. They are mostly place-names: as Dunharrow (for *Dúnharg*), except Shadowfax and Wormtongue.

II
WRITING

The scripts and letters used in the Third Age were all ultimately of Eldarin origin, and already at that time of great antiquity. They had reached the stage of full alphabetic development, but older modes in which only the consonants were denoted by full letters were still in use.

The alphabets were of two main, and in origin independent, kinds: the *Tengwar* or *Tîw*, here translated as 'letters'; and the *Certar* or *Cirth*, translated as 'runes'. The *Tengwar* were devised for writing with brush or pen, and the squared forms of inscriptions were in their case derivative from the written forms. The *Certar* were devised and mostly used only for scratched or incised inscriptions.

The *Tengwar* were the more ancient; for they had been developed by the Noldor, the kindred of the Eldar most skilled in such matters, long before their exile. The oldest Eldarin letters, the Tengwar of Rúmil, were not used in Middle-earth. The later letters, the Tengwar of Fëanor, were largely a new invention, though they owed something to the letters of Rúmil. They were brought to Middle-earth by the exiled Noldor, and so became known to the Edain and Númenoreans. In the Third Age their use had spread over much the same area as that in which the Common Speech was known.

The Cirth were devised first in Beleriand by the Sindar, and were long used only for inscribing names and brief memorials upon wood or stone. To that origin they owe their angular shapes, very similar to the runes of our times, though they differed from these in details and were wholly different in arrangement. The Cirth in their older and simpler form spread eastward in the Second Age, and became known to many peoples, to Men and Dwarves, and even to Orcs, all of whom altered them to suit their purposes and according to their skill or lack of it. One such simple form was still used by the Men of Dale, and a similar one by the Rohirrim.

But in Beleriand, before the end of the First Age, the Cirth, partly under the influence of the Tengwar of the Noldor, were rearranged and further developed. Their richest and most ordered form was known as the Alphabet of Daeron, since in Elvish tradition it was said to have been devised by Daeron, the minstrel and loremaster of King Thingol of Doriath. Among the Eldar the Alphabet of Daeron did not develop true cursive forms, since for writing the Elves adopted the Fëanorian letters. The Elves of the West indeed for the most part gave up the use of runes altogether. In the country of Eregion, however, the Alphabet of Daeron was maintained in use and passed thence to Moria, where it became the alphabet most favoured by the Dwarves. It remained ever after in use among them and passed with them to the North. Hence in later times it was often called *Angerthas Moria* or the Long Rune-rows of Moria. As with their speech the Dwarves made use of such scripts as were current and many wrote the Fëanorian letters skilfully; but for their own tongue they adhered to the Cirth, and developed written pen-forms from them.

(i)
THE FËANORIAN LETTERS

The table shows, in formal book-hand shape, all the letters that were commonly used in the West-lands in the Third Age. The arrangement is the one most usual at the time, and the one in which the letters were then usually recited by name.

This script was not in origin an 'alphabet', that is, a haphazard series of letters, each with an independent value of its own, recited in a traditional order that has no reference either to their shapes or to their functions.[1] It was, rather, a system of conson-

---

[1] The only relation in our alphabet that would have appeared intelligible to the Eldar is that between P and B; and their separation from one another, and from F, M, V, would have seemed to them absurd.

THE TENGWAR

I	II	III	IV
1 p	2 p	3 �763	4 ᴎ
5	6	7	8
9	10	11	12
13	14	15	16
17	18	19	20
21	22	23	24
25	26	27	28
29	30	31	32
33	34	35	36

antal signs, of similar shapes and style, which could be adapted at choice or convenience to represent the consonants of languages observed (or devised) by the Eldar. None of the letters had in itself a fixed value; but certain relations between them were gradually recognized.

The system contained twenty-four primary letters, 1–24, arranged in four *témar* (series), each of which had six *tyeller* (grades). There were also 'additional letters', of which 25–36 are examples. Of these 27 and 29 are the only strictly independent letters; the remainder are modifications of other letters. There was also a number of *tehtar* (signs) of varied uses. These do not appear in the table.[1]

The *primary letters* were each formed of a *telco* (stem) and a *lúva* (bow). The forms seen in 1–4 were regarded as normal. The stem could be raised, as in 9–16; or reduced, as in 17–24. The bow could be open, as in Series I and III; or closed, as in II and IV; and in either case it could be doubled, as e.g. in 5–8.

The theoretic freedom of application had in the Third Age been modified by custom to this extent that Series I was generally applied to the dental or *t*-series (*tincotéma*), and II to the labials or *p*-series (*parmatéma*). The application of Series III and IV varied according to the requirements of different languages.

In languages like the Westron, which made much use of consonants[2] such as our *ch*, *j*, *sh*, Series III was usually applied to these; in which case Series IV was applied to the normal *k*-series (*calmatéma*). In Quenya, which possessed besides the *calmatéma* both a palatal series (*tyelpetéma*) and a labialized series (*quessetéma*), the palatals were represented by a Fëanorian diacritic denoting 'following *y*' (usually two underposed dots), while Series IV was a *kw*-series.

Within these general applications the following relations were also commonly observed. The normal letters, Grade 1, were applied to the 'voiceless stops': *t*, *p*, *k*, etc. The doubling of the

---

[1] Many of them appear in the examples on the title-page, and in the inscription on I, p. 66, transcribed on II, p. 51. They were mainly used to express vowel-sounds, in Quenya usually regarded as modifications of the accompanying consonant; or to express more briefly some of the most frequent consonant combinations.

[2] The representation of the sounds here is the same as that employed in transcription and described above, except that here *ch* represents the *ch* in English *church*; *j* represents the sound of English *j*, and *zh* the sound heard in *azure* and *occasion*.

bow indicated the addition of 'voice': thus if 1, 2, 3, 4=*t, p, ch, k* (or *t, p, k, kw*) then 5, 6, 7, 8 =*d, b, j, g* (or *d, b, g, gw*). The raising of the stem indicated the opening of the consonant to a 'spirant': thus assuming the above values for Grade 1, Grade 3 (9–12)=*th, f, sh, ch* (or *th, f, kh, khw/hw*), and Grade 4 (13–16)=*dh, v, zh, gh* (or *dh, v, gh, ghw/w*).

The original Fëanorian system also possessed a grade with extended stems, both above and below the line. These usually represented aspirated consonants (e.g. *t+h, p+h, k+h*), but might represent other consonantal variations required. They were not needed in the languages of the Third Age that used this script; but the extended forms were much used as variants (more clearly distinguished from Grade 1) of Grades 3 and 4.

Grade 5 (17–20) was usually applied to the nasal consonants: thus 17 and 18 were the most common signs for *n* and *m*. According to the principle observed above, Grade 6 should then have represented the voiceless nasals; but since such sounds (exemplified by Welsh *nh* or ancient English *hn*) were of very rare occurrence in the languages concerned, Grade 6 (21–24) was most often used for the weakest or 'semi-vocalic' consonants of each series. It consisted of the smallest and simplest shapes among the primary letters. Thus 21 was often used for a weak (untrilled) *r*, originally occurring in Quenya and regarded in the system of that language as the weakest consonant of the *tinco-téma*; 22 was widely used for *w*; where Series III was used as a palatal series 23 was commonly used as consonantal *y*.[1]

Since some of the consonants of Grade 4 tended to become weaker in pronunciation, and to approach or to merge with those of Grade 6 (as described above), many of the latter ceased to have a clear function in the Eldarin languages; and it was from these letters that the letters expressing vowels were largely derived.

---

[1] The inscription on the West-gate of Moria gives an example of a mode, used for the spelling of Sindarin, in which Grade 6 represented the simple nasals, but Grade 5 represented the double or long nasals much used in Sindarin: 17=*nn*, but 21=*n*.

NOTE

The standard spelling of Quenya diverged from the applications of the letters above described. Grade 2 was used for *nd*, *mb*, *ng*, *ngw*, all of which were frequent, since *b*, *g*, *gw* only appeared in these combinations, while for *rd*, *ld* the special letters 26, 28 were used. (For *lv*, not for *lw*, many speakers, especially Elves, used *lb*: this was written with 27+6, since *lmb* could not occur.) Similarly, Grade 4 was used for the extremely frequent combinations *nt*, *mp*, *nk*, *nqu*, since Quenya did not possess *dh*, *gh*, *ghw*, and for *v* used letter 22. See the Quenya letter-names pp. 126–7.

The additional letters. No. 27 was universally used for *l*. No. 25 (in origin a modification of 21) was used for 'full' trilled *r*. Nos. 26, 28 were modifications of these. They were frequently used for voiceless *r* (*rh*) and *l* (*lh*) respectively. But in Quenya they were used for *rd* and *ld*. 29 represented *s*, and 31 (with doubled curl) *z* in those languages that required it. The inverted forms, 30 and 32, though available for use as separate signs, were mostly used as mere variants of 29 and 31, according to the convenience of writing, e.g. they were much used when accompanied by superimposed *tehtar*.

No. 33 was in origin a variation representing some (weaker) variety of 11; its most frequent use in the Third Age was *h*. 34 was mostly used (if at all) for voiceless *w* (*hw*). 35 and 36 were, when used as consonants, mostly applied to *y* and *w* respectively.

The vowels were in many modes represented by *tehtar*, usually set above a consonantal letter. In languages such as Quenya, in which most words ended in a vowel, the *tehta* was placed above the preceding consonant; in those such as Sindarin, in which most words ended in a consonant, it was placed above the following consonant. When there was no consonant present in the required position, the *tehta* was placed above the 'short carrier', of which a common form was like an undotted i. The actual *tehtar* used in different languages for vowel-signs were numerous. The commonest, usually applied to (varieties of) *e*, *i*, *a*, *o*, *u*, are exhibited in the examples given. The three dots, most usual in formal writing for *a*, were variously written in quicker styles, a form like a circumflex being often employed.[1] The single dot and the 'acute accent' were frequently used for *i* and *e* (but in some modes for *e* and *i*). The curls were used for *o* and *u*. In the Ring-inscription the curl open to the right is used for *u*; but on the title-page this stands for *o*, and the curl open to the left for *u*. The curl to the right was favoured, and the application depended on the language concerned: in the Black Speech *o* was rare.

Long vowels were usually represented by placing the *tehta* on the 'long carrier', of which a common form was like an undotted *j*. But for the same purpose the *tehtar* could be doubled. This was, however, only frequently done with the curls, and sometimes with the 'accent'. Two dots was more often used as a sign for following *y*.

The West-gate inscription illustrates a mode of 'full writing' with the vowels represented by separate letters. All the vocalic letters used in Sindarin are shown. The use of No. 30 as a sign for vocalic *y* may be noted; also the expression of diphthongs by placing the *tehta* for following *y* above the vowel-letter. The sign for following *w* (required for the expression of *au*, *aw*) was in this mode the *u*-curl or a modification of it ∼. But the diphthongs were often written out in full, as in the transcription. In this mode length of vowel was usually indicated by the 'acute accent', called in that case *andaith* 'long mark'.

There were beside the *tehtar* already mentioned a number of others, chiefly used to abbreviate the writing, especially by expressing frequent consonant combinations without writing them out in full. Among these, a bar (or a sign like a Spanish *tilde*) placed above a consonant was often used to indicate that it was preceded by the nasal of the same series (as in *nt*, *mp*, or *nk*); a similar sign placed below was, however, mainly used to show that the consonant was long or doubled. A downward hook attached to the bow (as in *hobbits*, the last word on the title-page)

---

[1] In Quenya in which *a* was very frequent, its vowel sign was often omitted altogether. Thus for *calma* 'lamp' *clm* could be written. This would naturally read as *calma*, since *cl* was not in Quenya a possible initial combination, and *m* never occurred finally. A possible reading was *calama*, but no such word existed.

was used to indicate a following *s*, especially in the combinations *ts*, *ps*, *ks* (*x*), that were favoured in Quenya.

There was of course no 'mode' for the representation of English. One adequate phonetically could be devised from the Fëanorian system. The brief example on the title-page does not attempt to exhibit this. It is rather an example of what a man of Gondor might have produced, hesitating between the values of the letters familiar in his 'mode' and the traditional spelling of English. It may be noted that a dot below (one of the uses of which was to represent weak obscured vowels) is here employed in the representation of unstressed *and*, but is also used in *here* for silent final *e*; *the*, *of*, and *of the* are expressed by abbreviations (extended *dh*, extended *v*, and the latter with an under-stroke).

The names of the letters. In all modes each letter and sign had a name; but these names were devised to fit or describe the phonetic uses in each particular mode. It was, however, often felt desirable, especially in describing the uses of the letters in other modes, to have a name for each letter in itself as a shape. For this purpose the Quenya 'full names' were commonly employed, even where they referred to uses peculiar to Quenya. Each 'full name' was an actual word in Quenya that contained the letter in question. Where possible it was the first sound of the word; but where the sound or the combination expressed did not occur initially it followed immediately after an initial vowel. The names of the letters in the table were (1) *tinco* metal, *parma* book, *calma* lamp, *quesse* feather; (2) *ando* gate, *umbar* fate, *anga* iron, *ungwe* spider's web; (3) *thúle* (*súle*) spirit, *formen* north, *harma* treasure (or *aha* rage), *hwesta* breeze; (4) *anto* mouth, *ampa* hook, *anca* jaws, *unque* a hollow; (5) *númen* west, *malta* gold, *noldo* (older *ngoldo*) one of the kindred of the Noldor, *nwalme* (older *ngwalme*) torment; (6) *óre* heart (inner mind), *vala* angelic power, *anna* gift, *vilya* air, sky (older *wilya*); *rómen* east, *arda* region, *lambe* tongue, *alda* tree; *silme* light, *silme nuquerna* (*s* reversed), *áre* sunlight (or *esse* name), *áre nuquerna*; *hyarmen* south, *hwesta sindarinwa*, *yanta* bridge, *úre* heat. Where there are variants this is due to the names being given before certain changes affected Quenya as spoken by the Exiles. Thus No. 11 was called *harma* when it represented the spirant *ch* in all positions, but when this sound became breath *h* initially[1] (though remaining medially) the name *aha* was devised. *áre* was originally *áze*, but when this *z* became merged with 21, the sign was in Quenya used for the very frequent *ss* of that language, and the name *esse* was given to it. *hwesta sindarinwa* or 'Grey-elven *hw*' was so called because in Quenya 12 had the sound of *hw*, and distinct signs for *chw* and *hw* were not required. The names of the letters most widely known and used were 17 *n*, 33 *hy*, 25 *r*, 9 *f*: *númen, hyarmen, rómen, formen*=west, south, east, north (cf. Sindarin *dûn* or *annûn, harad, rhûn* or *amrûn, forod*). These letters commonly indicated the points W, S, E, N even in languages that used quite different terms. They were, in the West-lands, named in this order, beginning with and facing west; *hyarmen* and *formen* indeed meant left-hand region and right-hand region (the opposite to the arrangement in many Mannish languages).

THE CIRTH

The *Certhas Daeron* was originally devised to represent the sounds of Sindarin only. The oldest *cirth* were Nos. 1, 2, 5, 6; 8, 9, 12; 18, 19, 22; 29, 31; 35, 36; 39, 42, 46, 50; and a *certh* varying between 13 and 15. The assignment of values was unsystematic. Nos. 39, 42, 46, 50 were vowels and remained so in all later developments. Nos. 13, 15 were used for *h* or *s*, according as 35 was used for *s* or *h*. This tendency to hesitate in the assignment of values for *s* and *h* continued in later arrangements. In those characters that consisted of a 'stem' and a 'branch', 1–31, the attachment of the branch was, if on one side only, usually made on the right side. The reverse was not infrequent, but had no phonetic significance.

---

[1] For breath *h* Quenya originally used a simple raised stem without bow, called *halla* 'tall'. This could be placed before a consonant to indicate that it was unvoiced and breathed; voiceless *r* and *l* were usually so expressed and are transcribed *hr, hl*. Later 33 was used for independent *h*, and the value of *hy* (its older value) was represented by adding the *tehta* for following *y*.

The extension and elaboration of this *certhas* was called in its older form the *Angerthas Daeron*, since the additions to the old *cirth* and their reorganization was attributed to Daeron. The principal additions, however, the introductions of two new series, 13–17, and 23–28, were actually most probably inventions of the Noldor of Eregion, since they were used for the representation of sounds not found in Sindarin.

In the rearrangement of the *Angerthas* the following principles are observable (evidently inspired by the Fëanorian system): (1) adding a stroke to a branch added 'voice'; (2) reversing the *certh* indicated opening to a 'spirant'; (3) placing the branch on both sides of the stem added voice and nasality. These principles were regularly carried out, except in one point. For (archaic) Sindarin a sign for a spirant *m* (or nasal *v*) was required, and since this could best be provided by a reversal of the sign for *m*, the reversible No. 6 was given the value *m*, but No. 5 was given the value *hw*.

No. 36, the theoretic value of which was *z*, was used, in spelling Sindarin or Quenya, for *ss*: cf. Fëanorian 31. No. 39 was used for either *i* or *y* (consonant); 34, 35 were used indifferently for *s*; and 38 was used for the frequent sequence *nd*, though it was not clearly related in shape to the dentals.

In the Table of Values those on the left are, when separated by – , the values of the older *Angerthas*. Those on the right are the values of the Dwarvish *Angerthas Moria*.[1] The Dwarves of Moria, as can be seen, introduced a number of unsystematic changes in value, as well as certain new *cirth*: 37, 40, 41, 53, 55, 56. The dislocation in values was due mainly to two causes: (1) the alteration in the values of 34, 35, 54 respectively to *h*,' (the clear or glottal beginning of a word with an initial vowel that appeared in Khuzdul), and *s*; (2) the abandonment of the Nos. 14, 16 for which the Dwarves substituted 29, 30. The consequent use of 12 for *r*, the invention of 53 for *n* (and its confusion with 22); the use of 17 as *z*, to go with 54 in its value *s*, and the consequent use of 36 as *ŋ* and the new *certh* 37 for *ng* may also be observed.

[1] Those in ( ) are values only found in Elvish use; * marks *cirth* only used by Dwarves.

The new 55, 56 were in origin a halved form of 46, and were used for vowels like those heard in English *butter*, which were frequent in Dwarvish and in the Westron. When weak or evanescent they were often reduced to a mere stroke without a stem. This *Angerthas Moria* is represented in the tomb-inscription.

The Dwarves of Erebor used a further modification of this system, known as the mode of Erebor, and exemplified in the Book of Mazarbul. Its chief characteristics were: the use of 43 as *z*; of 17 as *ks* (*x*); and the invention of two new *cirth*, 57, 58 for *ps* and *ts*. They also reintroduced 14, 16 for the values *j*, *zh*; but used 29, 30 for *g*, *gh*, or as mere variants of 19, 21. These peculiarities are not included in the table, except for the special Ereborian *cirth*, 57, 58.

THE ANGERTHAS

1	16	31	46
2	17	32	47
3	18	33	48
4	19	34	49
5	20	35	50
6	21	36	51
7	22	37	52
8	23	38	53
9	24	39	54
10	25	40	55
11	26	41	56
12	27	42	57
13	28	43	58
14	29	44	&
15	30	45	

THE ANGERTHAS

Values

1 p	16 zh	31 l	46 e
2 b	17 nj—z	32 lh	47 ē
3 f	18 k	33 ng—nd	48 a
4 v	19 g	34 s—h	49 ā
5 hw	20 kh	35 s—'	50 o
6 m	21 gh	36 z—ŋ	51 ð
7 (mh) mb	22 ŋ—n	37 ng*	52 ö
8 t	23 kw	38 nd—nj	53 n*
9 d	24 gw	39 i (y)	54 h—s
10 th	25 khw	40 y*	55 *
11 dh	26 ghw,w	41 hy*	56 *
12 n—r	27 ngw	42 u	57 ps*
13 ch	28 nw	43 ū	58 ts*
14 j	29 r—j	44 w	+h
15 sh	30 rh—zh	45 ü	&

APPENDIX F

I

THE LANGUAGES AND PEOPLES OF THE THIRD AGE

The language represented in this history by English was the *Westron* or 'Common Speech' of the West-lands of Middle-earth in the Third Age. In the course of that age it had become the native language of nearly all the speaking-peoples (save the Elves) who dwelt within the bounds of the old kingdoms of Arnor and Gondor; that is along all the coasts from Umbar northward to the Bay of Forochel, and inland as far as the Misty Mountains and the Ephel Dúath. It had also spread north up the Anduin, occupying the lands west of the River and east of the mountains as far as the Gladden Fields.

At the time of the War of the Ring at the end of the age these were still its bounds as a native tongue, though large parts of Eriador were now deserted, and few Men dwelt on the shores of the Anduin between the Gladden and Rauros.

A few of the ancient Wild Men still lurked in the Drúadan Forest in Anórien; and in the hills of Dunland a remnant lingered of an old people, the former inhabitants of much of Gondor. These clung to their own languages; while in the plains of Rohan there dwelt now a Northern people, the Rohirrim, who had come into that land some five hundred years earlier. But the Westron was used as a second language of intercourse by all those who still retained a speech of their own, even by the Elves, not only in Arnor and Gondor but throughout the vales of Anduin, and eastward to the further eaves of Mirkwood. Even among the Wild Men and the Dunlendings who shunned other folk there were some that could speak it, though brokenly.

OF THE ELVES

The Elves far back in the Elder Days became divided into two main branches: the West-elves (the *Eldar*) and the East-elves. Of the latter kind were most of the elven-folk of Mirkwood and Lórien; but their languages do not appear in this history, in which all the Elvish names and words are of *Eldarin* form.[1]

Of the *Eldarin* tongues two are found in this book: the High-elven or *Quenya*, and the Grey-elven or *Sindarin*. The High-elven was an ancient tongue of Eldamar beyond the Sea, the first to be recorded in writing. It was no longer a birth-tongue, but had become, as it were, an 'Elven-latin', still used for cere-mony, and for high matters of lore and song, by the High Elves, who had returned in exile to Middle-earth at the end of the First Age.

The Grey-elven was in origin akin to *Quenya*; for it was the language of those Eldar who, coming to the shores of Middle-earth, had not passed over the Sea but had lingered on the coasts in the country of Beleriand. There Thingol Greycloak of Doriath was their king, and in the long twilight their tongue had changed with the changefulness of mortal lands and had become far estranged from the speech of the Eldar from beyond the Sea.

The Exiles, dwelling among the more numerous Grey-elves, had adopted the *Sindarin* for daily use; and hence it was the tongue of all those Elves and Elf-lords that appear in this history. For these were all of Eldarin race, even where the folk that they ruled were of the lesser kindreds. Noblest of all was the Lady Galadriel of the royal house of Finarfin and sister of Finrod Felagund, King of Nargothrond. In the hearts of the Exiles the yearning for the Sea was an unquiet never to be stilled; in the hearts of the Grey-elves it slumbered, but once awakened it could not be appeased.

[1] In Lórien at this period Sindarin was spoken, though with an 'accent', since most of its folk were of Silvan origin. This 'accent' and his own limited acquaintance with Sindarin misled Frodo (as is pointed out in *The Thain's Book* by a commentator of Gondor). All the Elvish words cited in Book II, chs 6, 7, 8 are in fact Sindarin, and so are most of the names of places and persons. But *Lórien, Caras Galadhon, Amroth, Nimrodel* are probably of Silvan origin, adapted to Sindarin.

OF MEN

The *Westron* was a Mannish speech, though enriched and soft-
ened under Elvish influence. It was in origin the language of
those whom the Eldar called the *Atani* or *Edain*, 'Fathers of
Men', being especially the people of the Three Houses of the
Elf-friends who came west into Beleriand in the First Age, and
aided the Eldar in the War of the Great Jewels against the Dark
Power of the North.

After the overthrow of the Dark Power, in which Beleriand
was for the most part drowned or broken, it was granted as a
reward to the Elf-friends that they also, as the Eldar, might pass
west over Sea. But since the Undying Realm was forbidden to
them, a great isle was set apart for them, most westerly of all
mortal lands. The name of that isle was *Númenor* (Westernesse).
Most of the Elf-friends, therefore, departed and dwelt in
Númenor, and there they became great and powerful, mariners
of renown and lords of many ships. They were fair of face and
tall, and the span of their lives was thrice that of the Men of
Middle-earth. These were the Númenoreans, the Kings of Men,
whom the Elves called the *Dúnedain*.

The *Dúnedain* alone of all races of Men knew and spoke an
Elvish tongue; for their forefathers had learned the Sindarin
tongue, and this they handed on to their children as a matter of
lore, changing little with the passing of the years. And their men
of wisdom learned also the High-elven Quenya and esteemed it
above all other tongues, and in it they made names for many
places of fame and reverence, and for many men of royalty and
great renown.[1]

But the native speech of the Númenoreans remained for the
most part their ancestral Mannish tongue, the Adûnaic, and to
this in the latter days of their pride their kings and lords returned,

---

[1] Quenya, for example, are the names *Númenor* (or in full *Númenóre*),
and *Elendil, Isildur,* and *Anárion,* and all the royal names of *Gondor,*
including *Elessar* 'Elfstone'. Most of the names of the other men and
women of the Dúnedain, such as *Aragorn, Denethor, Gilraen* are of Sindarin form, being often the names of Elves or Men remembered in the
songs and histories of the First Age (as *Beren, Húrin*). Some few are of
mixed forms, as *Boromir.*

abandoning the Elven-speech, save only those few that held still to their ancient friendship with the Eldar. In the years of their power the Númenoreans had maintained many forts and havens upon the western coasts of Middle-earth for the help of their ships; and one of the chief of these was at Pelargir near the Mouths of Anduin. There Adûnaic was spoken, and mingled with many words of the languages of lesser men it became a Common Speech that spread thence along the coasts among all that had dealings with Westernesse.

After the Downfall of Númenor, Elendil led the survivors of the Elf-friends back to the North-western shores of Middle-earth. There many already dwelt who were in whole or part of Númenorean blood; but few of them remembered the Elvish speech. All told the Dúnedain were thus from the beginning far fewer in number than the lesser men among whom they dwelt and whom they ruled, being lords of long life and great power and wisdom. They used therefore the Common Speech in their dealing with other folk and in the government of their wide realms; but they enlarged the language and enriched it with many words drawn from Elven-tongues.

In the days of the Númenorean kings this ennobled Westron speech spread far and wide, even among their enemies; and it became used more and more by the Dúnedain themselves, so that at the time of the War of the Ring the Elven-tongue was known to only a small part of the peoples of Gondor, and spoken daily by fewer. These dwelt mostly in Minas Tirith and the townlands adjacent, and in the land of the tributary princes of Dol Amroth. Yet the names of nearly all places and persons in the realm of Gondor were of Elvish form and meaning. A few were of forgotten origin, and descended doubtless from the days before the ships of the Númenoreans sailed the Sea; among these were *Umbar*, *Arnach* and *Erech*; and the mountain-names *Eilenach* and *Rimmon*. *Forlong* was also a name of the same sort.

Most of the Men of the northern regions of the West-lands were descended from the *Edain* of the First Age, or from their close kin. Their languages were, therefore, related to the Adûnaic, and some still preserved a likeness to the Common Speech. Of this kind were the peoples of the upper vales of Anduin: the Beornings, and the Woodmen of Western Mirkwood; and further north and east the Men of the Long Lake and of Dale. From the lands between the Gladden and the Carrock came the folk that were known in Gondor as the Rohirrim, Masters of Horses. They still spoke their ancestral tongue, and gave new names in it to nearly all the places in their new country; and they called themselves the Eorlings, or the Men of the Rid-dermark. But the lords of that people used the Common Speech freely, and spoke it nobly after the manner of their allies in Gondor; for in Gondor whence it came the Westron kept still a more gracious and antique style.

Wholly alien was the speech of the Wild Men of Drúadan Forest. Alien, too, or only remotely akin, was the language of the Dunlendings. These were a remnant of the peoples that had dwelt in the vales of the White Mountains in ages past. The Dead Men of Dunharrow were of their kin. But in the Dark Years others had removed to the southern dales of the Misty Mountains; and thence some had passed into the empty lands as far north as the Barrow-downs. From them came the Men of Bree; but long before these had become subjects of the North Kingdom of Arnor and had taken up the Westron tongue. Only in Dunland did Men of this race hold to their old speech and manners: a secret folk, unfriendly to the Dúnedain, hating the Rohirrim.

Of their language nothing appears in this book, save the name *Forgoil* which they gave to the Rohirrim (meaning Strawheads, it is said). *Dunland* and *Dunlending* are the names that the Rohir-rim gave to them, because they were swarthy and dark-haired; there is thus no connexion between the word *dunn* in these names and the Grey-elven word *Dûn* 'west'.

OF HOBBITS

The Hobbits of the Shire and of Bree had at this time, for probably a thousand years, adopted the Common Speech. They used it in their own manner freely and carelessly; though the more learned among them had still at their command a more formal language when occasion required.

There is no record of any language peculiar to Hobbits. In ancient days they seem always to have used the languages of

Men near whom, or among whom, they lived. Thus they quickly adopted the Common Speech after they entered Eriador, and by the time of their settlement at Bree they had already begun to forget their former tongue. This was evidently a Mannish language of the upper Anduin, akin to that of the Rohirrim; though the southern Stoors appear to have adopted a language related to Dunlendish before they came north to the Shire.[1]

Of these things in the time of Frodo there were still some traces left in local words and names, many of which closely resembled those found in Dale or in Rohan. Most notable were the names of days, months, and seasons; several other words of the same sort (such as *mathom* and *smial*) were also still in common use, while more were preserved in the place-names of Bree and the Shire. The personal names of the Hobbits were also peculiar and many had come down from ancient days.

Hobbit was the name usually applied by the Shire-folk to all their kind. Men called them *Halflings* and the Elves *Periannath*. The origin of the word *hobbit* was by most forgotten. It seems, however, to have been at first a name given to the Harfoots by the Fallohides and Stoors, and to be a worn-down form of a word preserved more fully in Rohan: *holbytla* 'hole-builder'.

OF OTHER RACES

Ents. The most ancient people surviving in the Third Age were the *Onodrim* or *Enyd*. *Ent* was the form of their name in the language of Rohan. They were known to the Eldar in ancient days, and to the Eldar indeed the Ents ascribed not their own language but the desire for speech. The language that they had made was unlike all others: slow, sonorous, agglomerated, repetitive, indeed long-winded; formed of a multiplicity of vowel-shades and distinctions of tone and quality which even the lore-masters of the Eldar had not attempted to represent in writing. They used it only among themselves; but they had no need to keep it secret, for no others could learn it.

---

[1] The Stoors of the Angle, who returned to Wilderland, had already adopted the Common Speech; but *Déagol* and *Sméagol* are names in the Mannish language of the region near the Gladden.

Ents were, however, themselves skilled in tongues, learning them swiftly and never forgetting them. But they preferred the languages of the Eldar, and loved best the ancient High-elven tongue. The strange words and names that the Hobbits record as used by Treebeard and other Ents are thus Elvish, or fragments of Elf-speech strung together in Ent-fashion.[1] Some are Quenya: as *Taurelilómëa-tumbalemorna Tumbaletaurëa Lómëanor,* which may be rendered 'Forestmanyshadowed-deepvalleyblack Deepvalleyforested Gloomyland', and by which Treebeard meant, more or less: 'there is a black shadow in the deep dales of the forest'. Some are Sindarin: as *Fangorn* 'beard-(of)-tree', or *Fimbrethil* 'slender-beech'.

Orcs and the Black Speech. Orc is the form of the name that other races had for this foul people as it was in the language of Rohan. In Sindarin it was *orch*. Related, no doubt, was the word *uruk* of the Black Speech, though this was applied as a rule only to the great soldier-orcs that at this time issued from Mordor and Isengard. The lesser kinds were called, especially by the Uruk-hai, *snaga* 'slave'.

The Orcs were first bred by the Dark Power of the North in the Elder Days. It is said that they had no language of their own, but took what they could of other tongues and perverted it to their own liking; yet they made only brutal jargons, scarcely sufficient even for their own needs, unless it were for curses and abuse. And these creatures, being filled with malice, hating even their own kind, quickly developed as many barbarous dialects as there were groups or settlements of their race, so that their Orkish speech was of little use to them in intercourse between different tribes.

So it was that in the Third Age Orcs used for communication between breed and breed the Westron tongue; and many indeed of the older tribes, such as those that still lingered in the North

---

[1] Except where the Hobbits seem to have made some attempts to represent shorter murmurs and calls made by the Ents; *a-lalla-lalla-rumba-kamanda-lindor-burúme* also is not Elvish, and is the only extant (probably very inaccurate) attempt to represent a fragment of actual Entish.

and in the Misty Mountains, had long used the Westron as their native language, though in such a fashion as to make it hardly less unlovely than Orkish. In this jargon *tark*, 'man of Gondor', was a debased form of *tarkil*, a Quenya word used in Westron for one of Númenorean descent; see VI, p. 17.

It is said that the Black Speech was devised by Sauron in the Dark Years, and that he had desired to make it the language of all those that served him, but he failed in that purpose. From the Black Speech, however, were derived many of the words that were in the Third Age wide-spread among the Orcs, such as *ghâsh* 'fire', but after the first overthrow of Sauron this language in its ancient form was forgotten by all but the Nazgûl. When Sauron arose again, it became once more the language of Barad-dûr and of the captains of Mordor. The inscription on the Ring was in the ancient Black Speech, while the curse of the Mordor-orc on III, p. 47 was in the more debased form used by the soldiers of the Dark Tower, of whom Grishnákh was the captain. *Sharkū* in that tongue means *old man*.

Trolls. Troll has been used to translate the Sindarin *Torog*. In their beginning far back in the twilight of the Elder Days, these were creatures of dull and lumpish nature and had no more language than beasts. But Sauron had made use of them, teaching them what little they could learn and increasing their wits with wickedness. Trolls therefore took such language as they could master from the Orcs; and in the Westlands the Stone-trolls spoke a debased form of the Common Speech.

But at the end of the Third Age a troll-race not before seen appeared in southern Mirkwood and in the mountain borders of Mordor. Olog-hai they were called in the Black Speech. That Sauron bred them none doubted, though from what stock was not known. Some held that they were not Trolls but giant Orcs; but the Olog-hai were in fashion of body and mind quite unlike even the largest of Orc-kind, whom they far surpassed in size and power. Trolls they were, but filled with the evil will of their master: a fell race, strong, agile, fierce and cunning, but harder than stone. Unlike the older race of the Twilight they could endure the Sun, so long as the will of Sauron held sway over them. They spoke little, and the only tongue that they knew was the Black Speech of Barad-dûr.

Dwarves. The Dwarves are a race apart. Of their strange beginning, and why they are both like and unlike Elves and Men, the Silmarillion tells; but of this tale the lesser Elves of Middle-earth had no knowledge, while the tales of later Men are confused with memories of other races.

They are a tough, thrawn race for the most part, secretive, laborious, retentive of the memory of injuries (and of benefits), lovers of stone, of gems, of things that take shape under the hands of the craftsman rather than things that live by their own life. But they are not evil by nature, and few ever served the Enemy of free will, whatever the tales of Men may have alleged. For Men of old lusted after their wealth and the work of their hands, and there has been enmity between the races.

But in the Third Age close friendship still was found in many places between Men and Dwarves; and it was according to the nature of the Dwarves that, travelling and labouring and trading about the lands, as they did after the destruction of their ancient mansions, they should use the languages of Men among whom they dwelt. Yet in secret (a secret which unlike the Elves, they did not willingly unlock, even to their friends) they used their own strange tongue, changed little by the years; for it had become a tongue of lore rather than a cradle-speech, and they tended it and guarded it as a treasure of the past. Few of other race have succeeded in learning it. In this history it appears only in such place-names as Gimli revealed to his companions; and in the battle-cry which he uttered in the siege of the Hornburg. That at least was not secret, and had been heard on many a field since the world was young. *Baruk Khazâd! Khazâd ai-mênu!* 'Axes of the Dwarves! The Dwarves are upon you!'

Gimli's own name, however, and the names of all his kin, are of Northern (Mannish) origin. Their own secret and 'inner' names, their true names, the Dwarves have never revealed to any one of alien race. Not even on their tombs do they inscribe them.

II
ON TRANSLATION

In presenting the matter of the Red Book, as a history for people of today to read, the whole of the linguistic setting has been translated as far as possible into terms of our own times. Only the languages alien to the Common Speech have been left in their original form; but these appear mainly in the names of persons and places.

The Common Speech, as the language of the Hobbits and their narratives, has inevitably been turned into modern English. In the process the difference between the varieties observable in the use of the Westron has been lessened. Some attempt has been made to represent varieties by variations in the kind of English used; but the divergence between the pronunciation and idiom of the Shire and the Westron tongue in the mouths of the Elves or of the high men of Gondor was greater than has been shown in this book. Hobbits indeed spoke for the most part a rustic dialect, whereas in Gondor and Rohan a more antique language was used, more formal and more terse.

One point in the divergence may here be noted, since, though important, it has proved impossible to represent. The Westron tongue made in the pronouns of the second person (and often also in those of the third) a distinction, independent of number, between 'familiar' and 'deferential' forms. It was, however, one of the peculiarities of Shire-usage that the deferential forms had gone out of colloquial use. They lingered only among the villagers, especially of the Westfarthing, who used them as endearments. This was one of the things referred to when people of Gondor spoke of the strangeness of Hobbit-speech. Peregrin Took, for instance, in his first few days in Minas Tirith used the familiar for people of all ranks, including the Lord Denethor himself. This may have amused the aged Steward, but it must have astonished his servants. No doubt this free use of the familiar forms helped to spread the popular rumour that Peregrin was a person of very high rank in his own country.[1]

---

[1] In one or two places an attempt has been made to hint at these distinctions by an inconsistent use of *thou*. Since this pronoun is now

It will be noticed that Hobbits such as Frodo, and other persons such as Gandalf and Aragorn, do not always use the same style. This is intentional. The more learned and able among the Hobbits had some knowledge of 'book-language', as it was termed in the Shire; and they were quick to note and adopt the style of those whom they met. It was in any case natural for much-travelled folk to speak more or less after the manner of those among whom they found themselves, especially in the case of men who, like Aragorn, were often at pains to conceal their origin and their business. Yet in those days all the enemies of the Enemy revered what was ancient, in language no less than in other matters, and they took pleasure in it according to their knowledge. The Eldar, being above all skilled in words, had the command of many styles, though they spoke most naturally in a manner nearest to their own speech, one even more antique than that of Gondor. The Dwarves, too, spoke with skill, readily adapting themselves to their company, though their utterance seemed to some rather harsh and guttural. But Orcs and Trolls spoke as they would, without love of words or things; and their language was actually more degraded and filthy than I have shown it. I do not suppose that any will wish for a closer rendering, though models are easy to find. Much the same sort of talk can still be heard among the orc-minded; dreary and repetitive with hatred and contempt, too long removed from good to retain even verbal vigour, save in the ears of those to whom only the squalid sounds strong.

Translation of this kind is, of course, usual because inevitable in any narrative dealing with the past. It seldom proceeds any further. But I have gone beyond it. I have also translated all Westron names according to their senses. When English names or titles appear in this book it is an indication that names in the Common Speech were current at the time, beside, or instead of, those in alien (usually Elvish) languages.

---

unusual and archaic it is employed mainly to represent the use of cere-monious language; but a change from *you* to *thou*, *thee* is sometimes meant to show, there being no other means of doing this, a significant change from the deferential, or between men and women normal, forms to the familiar.

The Westron names were as a rule translations of older names: as Rivendell, Hoarwell, Silverlode, Langstrand, The Enemy, the Dark Tower. Some differed in meaning: as Mount Doom for *Orodruin* 'burning mountain', or Mirkwood for *Taur e-Ndaedelos* 'forest of great fear'. A few were alterations of Elvish names: as Lune and Brandywine derived from *Lhûn* and *Baranduin*.

This procedure perhaps needs some defence. It seemed to me that to present all the names in their original forms would obscure an essential feature of the times as perceived by the Hobbits (whose point of view I was mainly concerned to preserve): the contrast between a wide-spread language, to them as ordinary and habitual as English is to us, and the living remains of far older and more reverend tongues. All names if merely transcribed would seem to modern readers equally remote: for instance, if the Elvish name *Imladris* and the Westron translation *Karningul* had both been left unchanged. But to refer to Rivendell as Imladris was as if one now was to speak of Winchester as Camelot, except that the identity was certain, while in Rivendell there still dwelt a lord of renown far older than Arthur would be, were he still king at Winchester today.

The name of the Shire (*Sûza*) and all other places of the Hobbits have thus been Englished. This was seldom difficult, since such names were commonly made up of elements similar to those used in our simpler English place-names; either words still current like *hill* or *field*; or a little worn down like *ton* beside *town*. But some were derived, as already noted, from old hobbit-words no longer in use, and these have been represent by similar English things, such as *wich*, or *bottle* 'dwelling', or *michel* 'great'.

In the case of persons, however, Hobbit-names in the Shire and in Bree were for those days peculiar, notably in the habit that had grown up, some centuries before this time, of having inherited names for families. Most of these surnames had obvious meanings (in the current language being derived from jesting nicknames, or from place-names, or – especially in Bree – from the names of plants and trees). Translation of these presented little difficulty; but there remained one or two older names of forgotten meaning, and these I have been content to anglicize in spelling: as Took for *Tûk*, or Boffin for *Bophîn*.

I have treated Hobbit first-names, as far as possible, in the same way. To their maid-children Hobbits commonly gave the names of flowers or jewels. To their man-children they usually gave names that had no meaning at all in their daily language; and some of their women's names were similar. Of this kind are Bilbo, Bungo, Polo, Lotho, Tanta, Nina, and so on. There are many inevitable but accidental resemblances to names we now have or know: for instance Otho, Odo, Drogo, Dora, Cora, and the like. These names I have retained, though I have usually anglicized them by altering their endings, since in Hobbit-names *a* was a masculine ending, and *o* and *e* were feminine.

In some old families, especially those of Fallohide origin such as the Tooks and the Bolgers, it was, however, the custom to give high-sounding first-names. Since most of these seem to have been drawn from legends of the past, of Men as well as of Hobbits, and many while now meaningless to Hobbits closely resembled the names of Men in the Vale of Anduin, or in Dale, or in the Mark, I have turned them into those old names, largely of Frankish and Gothic origin, that are still used by us or are met in our histories. I have thus at any rate preserved the often comic contrast between the first-names and surnames, of which the Hobbits themselves were well aware. Names of classical origin have rarely been used; for the nearest equivalents to Latin and Greek in Shire-lore were the Elvish tongues, and these the Hobbits seldom used in nomenclature. Few of them at any time knew the 'languages of the kings', as they called them.

The names of the Bucklanders were different from those of· the rest of the Shire. The folk of the Marish and their offshoot across the Brandywine were in many ways peculiar, as has been told. It was from the former language of the southern Stoors, no doubt, that they inherited many of their very odd names. These I have usually left unaltered, for if queer now, they were queer in their own day. They had a style that we should perhaps feel vaguely to be 'Celtic'.

Since the survival of traces of the older language of the Stoors and the Bree-men resembled the survival of Celtic elements in England, I have sometimes imitated the latter in my translation. Thus Bree, Combe (Coomb), Archet, and Chetwood are modelled on relics of British nomenclature, chosen according to sense: *bree* 'hill' *chet* 'wood'. But only one personal name has been altered in this way. Meriadoc was chosen to fit the fact that this character's shortened name, Kali, meant in the Westron 'jolly, gay', though it was actually an abbreviation of the now unmeaning Buckland name Kalimac.

I have not used names of Hebraic or similar origin in my transpositions. Nothing in Hobbit-names corresponds to this element in our names. Short names such as Sam, Tom, Tim, Mat were common as abbreviations of actual Hobbit-names, such as Tomba, Tolma, Matta, and the like. But Sam and his father Ham were really called Ban and Ran. These were shortenings of *Banazîr* and *Ranugad*, originally nicknames, meaning 'halfwise, simple' and 'stay-at-home'; but being words that had fallen out of colloquial use they remained as traditional names in certain families. I have therefore tried to preserve these features by using Samwise and Hamfast, modernizations of ancient English *samwis* and *hámfoest* which corresponded closely in meaning.

Having gone so far in my attempt to modernize and make familiar the language and names of Hobbits, I found myself involved in a further process. The Mannish languages that were related to the Westron should, it seemed to me, be turned into forms related to English. The language of Rohan I have accordingly made to resemble ancient English, since it was related both (more distantly) to the Common Speech, and (very closely) to the former tongue of the northern Hobbits, and was in comparison with the Westron archaic. In the Red Book it is noted in several places that when Hobbits heard the speech of Rohan they recognized many words and felt the language to be akin to their own, so that it seemed absurd to leave the recorded names and words of the Rohirrim in a wholly alien style.

In several cases I have modernized the forms and spellings of place-names in Rohan: as in *Dunharrow* or *Snowbourn*; but I have not been consistent, for I have followed the Hobbits. They altered the names that they heard in the same way, if they were made of elements that they recognized, or if they resembled place-names in the Shire; but many they left alone, as I have done, for instance, in *Edoras* 'the courts'. For the same reasons a few personal names have also been modernized, as Shadowfax and Wormtongue.[1]

This assimilation also provided a convenient way of representing the peculiar local hobbit-words that were of northern origin. They have been given the forms that lost English words might well have had, if they had come down to our day. Thus *mathom* is meant to recall ancient English *máthm*, and so to represent the relationship of the actual Hobbit *kast* to R. *kastu*. Similarly *smial* (or *smile*) 'burrow' is a likely form for a descendant of *smygel*, and represents well the relationship of Hobbit *trân* to R. *trahan*. *Sméagol* and *Déagol* are equivalents made up in the same way for the names *Trahald* 'burrowing, worming in', and *Nahald* 'secret' in the Northern tongues.

The still more northerly language of Dale is in this book seen only in the names of the Dwarves that came from that region and so used the language of the Men there, taking their 'outer' names in that tongue. It may be observed that in this book as in *The Hobbit* the form *dwarves* is used, although the dictionaries tell us that the plural of *dwarf* is *dwarfs*. It should be *dwarrows* (or *dwerrows*), if singular and plural had each gone its own way down the years, as have *man* and *men*, or *goose* and *geese*. But we no longer speak of a dwarf as often as we do of a man, or even of a goose, and memories have not been fresh enough among Men to keep hold of a special plural for a race now abandoned to folk-tales, where at least a shadow of truth is preserved, or at last to nonsense-stories in which they have become mere figures of fun. But in the Third Age something of their old character and power is still glimpsed, if already a little dimmed; these are the descendants of the Naugrim of the Elder Days, in whose hearts still burns the ancient fire of Aulë the Smith, and the embers smoulder of their long grudge against the Elves; and in whose hands still lives the skill in work of stone that none have surpassed.

[1] This linguistic procedure does not imply that the Rohirrim closely resembled the ancient English otherwise, in culture or art, in weapons or modes of warfare, except in a general way due to their circumstances: a simpler and more primitive people living in contact with a higher and more venerable culture, and occupying lands that had once been part of its domain.

It is to mark this that I have ventured to use the form *dwarves*, and remove them a little, perhaps, from the sillier tales of these latter days. *Dwarrows* would have been better; but I have used that form only in the name *Dwarrowdelf*, to represent the name of Moria in the Common Speech: *Phurunargian*. For that meant 'Dwarf-delving' and yet was already a word of antique form. But Moria is an Elvish name, and given without love; for the Eldar, though they might at need, in their bitter wars with the Dark Power and his servants, contrive fortresses underground, were not dwellers in such places of choice. They were lovers of the green earth and the lights of heaven; and Moria in their tongue means the Black Chasm. But the Dwarves themselves, and this name at least was never kept secret, called it *Khazad-dûm*, the Mansion of the Khazâd; for such is their own name for their own race, and has been so, since Aulë gave it to them at their making in the deeps of time.

Elves has been used to translate both *Quendi*, 'the speakers', the High-elven name of all their kind, and *Eldar*, the name of the Three Kindreds that sought for the Undying Realm and came there at the beginning of Days (save the *Sindar* only). This old word was indeed the only one available, and was once fitted to apply to such memories of this people as Men preserved, or to the makings of Men's minds not wholly dissimilar. But it has been diminished, and to many it may now suggest fancies either pretty or silly, as unlike to the Quendi of old as are butterflies to the falcon – not that any of the Quendi ever possessed wings of the body, as unnatural to them as to Men. They were a race high and beautiful, the older Children of the world, and among them the Eldar were as kings, who now are gone: the People of the Great Journey, the People of the Stars. They were tall, fair of skin and grey-eyed, though their locks were dark, save in the golden house of Finarfin; and their voices had more melodies than any mortal voice that now is heard. They were valiant, but the history of those that returned to Middle-earth in exile was grievous; and though it was in far-off days crossed by the fate of the Fathers, their fate is not that of Men. Their dominion passed long ago, and they dwell now beyond the circles of the world, and do not return.

Note on three names: *Hobbit*, *Gamgee*, and *Brandywine*.

Hobbit is an invention. In the Westron the word used, when this people was referred to at all, was *banakil* 'halfling'. But at this date the folk of the Shire and of Bree used the word *kuduk*, which was not found elsewhere. Meriadoc, however, actually records that the King of Rohan used the word *kûd-dûkan* 'hole-dweller'. Since, as has been noted, the Hobbits had once spoken a language closely related to that of the Rohirrim, it seems likely that *kuduk* was a worn-down form of *kûd-dûkan*. The latter I have translated, for reasons explained, by *holbytla*; and *hobbit* provides a word that might well be a worn-down form of *holbytla*, if that name had occurred in our own ancient language.

Gamgee. According to family tradition, set out in the Red Book, the surname *Galbasi*, or in reduced form *Galpsi*, came from the village of *Galabas*, popularly supposed to be derived from *galab-* 'game' and an old element *bas-*, more or less equivalent to our *wick, wich. Gamwich* (pronounced *Gammidge*) seemed therefore a very fair rendering. However, in reducing *Gammidgy* to *Gamgee*, to represent *Galpsi*, no reference was intended to the connexion of Samwise with the family of Cotton, though a jest of that kind would have been hobbit-like enough, had there been any warrant in their language.

Cotton, in fact, represents *Hlothran*, a fairly common village-name in the Shire, derived from *hloth*, 'a two-roomed dwelling or hole', and *ran(u)* a small group of such dwellings on a hill-side. As a surname it may be an alteration of *hlothram(a)* 'cottager'. *Hlothram*, which I have rendered Cotman, was the name of Farmer Cotton's grandfather.

Brandywine. The hobbit-names of this river were alterations of the Elvish *Baranduin* (accented on *and*), derived from *baran* 'golden brown' and *duin* '(large) river'. Of *Baranduin* Brandywine seemed a natural corruption in modern times. Actually the older hobbit-name was *Branda-nîn* 'border-water', which would have been more closely rendered by Marchbourn; but by a jest that had become habitual, referring again to its colour, at this time the river was usually called *Bralda-hîm* 'heady ale'.

It must be observed, however, that when the Oldbucks (*Zaragamba*) changed their name to Brandybuck (*Brandagamba*), the first element meant 'borderland', and Marchbuck would have been nearer. Only a very bold hobbit would have ventured to call the Master of Buckland *Braldagamba* in his hearing.

INDEX

(b) First Lines

*All Tom Bombadil's songs are
treated, for index purposes, as
continuations of this one.

IV Things

MAPS

NOTE ON THE MAPS

Maps accompanying *The Lord of the Rings* were drawn by Christopher Tolkien for the original edition published in 1954–5. They consisted of a general map of the western regions of Middle-earth and a more detailed map of Rohan, Gondor, and Mordor; printed in red and black on large folded sheets pasted in at the end of each of the three books, *The Fellowship of the Ring* and *The Two Towers* carried the general map, while *The Return of the King* carried the other. In addition, there was a map of the Shire in red and black preceding Book I of *The Fellowship of the Ring*. Christopher Tolkien redrew the general map expressly for inclusion in *Unfinished Tales* (1980), but subsequently this replaced the original form in editions of *The Lord of the Rings*.

With paperback editions the arrangement was introduced whereby the general map was divided into four sections, in black only, fitting the size of the pages, while the whole map in greatly reduced form was also printed as a guide to the sections. The map of Rohan, Gondor, and Mordor was reduced to fit two facing pages. This arrangement is found in all current paperback and one-volume hardback editions.

The original maps, however, were not drawn and lettered in such a way as to make such reduction satisfactory. Mr Stephen Raw has therefore redrawn them all, very closely following the originals, and greatly increasing their clarity. As a guide to the four sections of the general map he has drawn a new outline map that provides all necessary indications in a simplified form.

THE WEST OF MIDDLE-EARTH

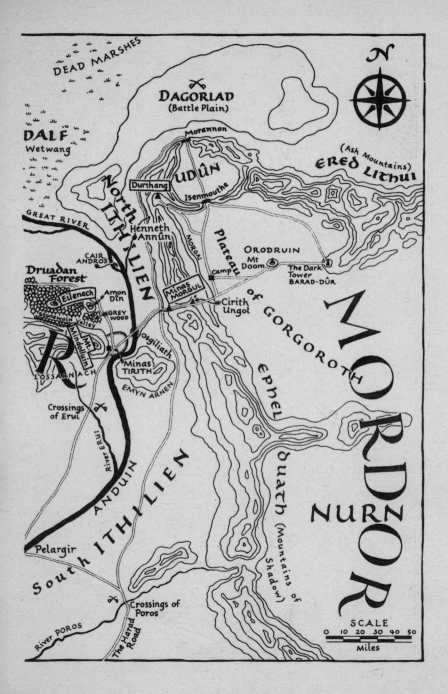